Bed-Knob
and
Broomstick

Bed-Knob and Broomstick

Mary Norton

ILLUSTRATED BY ERIK BLEGVAD

A Combined Edition of *The Magic Bed-Knob*
and *Bonfires and Broomsticks*

SCHOLASTIC INC.
New York Toronto London Auckland Sydney
Mexico City New Delhi Hong Kong Buenos Aires

ISBN 0-439-31481-X

Published by Scholastic Inc., 555 Broadway, New York, NY 10012,
by arrangement with Harcourt Inc.
SCHOLASTIC and associated logos are trademarks and/or
registered trademarks of Scholastic Inc.

12 11 10 9 8 7 6 5 4 3 2   1 2 3 4 5 6/0

Printed in the U.S.A.   40

First Scholastic printing, September 2001

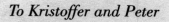

To Kristoffer and Peter

CONTENTS

I
The Magic Bed-Knob

II
Bonfires and Broomsticks

Bed-Knob
and
Broomstick

I

THE MAGIC BED-KNOB

1

How They Met Her

Once upon a time there were three children, and their names were Carey, Charles, and Paul. Carey was about your age, Charles a little younger, and Paul was only six.

One summer, they were sent to Bedfordshire to stay with an aunt. She was an old aunt and she lived in an old square house—which lay in a garden where no flowers grew. There were lawns and shrubs and cedars but no flowers, which made the garden seem grave and sad.

The children were shy of the house, with its big hall and wide stairways; they were shy of Elizabeth—the stern old housemaid—and they were shy of their aunt, too, because she had pale blue eyes with pinkish edges and did not often smile. But they loved the garden and river that ran through it and the countryside beyond with its tangled hedges and sweet meadow grass.

They were out all day.

They played in the barns, they played by the river, and they played in the lanes and on the hills. They were punctual for meals because they were visitors and good children at heart. One day slipped into another, and all the days were alike—until Miss Price hurt her ankle. And that's where the story begins.

You all know somebody rather like Miss Price. She wore gray coats and skirts and had a long thin neck with a scarf round it made of Liberty silk with a paisley pattern. Her nose was sharply pointed, and she had very clean, pink hands. She rode on a high bicycle with a basket in front, and she visited the sick and taught the piano. She lived in a neat little house that stood in a lane at the bottom of the garden, and the children knew her by sight and always said "Good morning." In all the village there was none so ladylike as Miss Price.

Now, one day, the children decided to go mushroom picking before breakfast. They awoke almost before the night had drained away from the sleeping house and tiptoed through the hall in their stocking feet. When they got outside, the garden was very still and drenched in dew, and, as they walked, their shoes left black smudges in the pearly grass. They spoke in whispers because it seemed as if the world, except the birds, were still asleep.

Suddenly, Paul stood still, staring down the slope of the lawn toward the darkness of the cedars. "What's that?"

They all stopped and they all stared.

"It moved," Paul told them. "Come on, let's see."

Carey sped ahead on her long legs. "It's a person," she called back, and then her step grew slower. She waited until they caught up with her. "It's—" Her voice was hushed with surprise. "It's Miss Price!"

And so it was, sitting there on the wet ground under the cedar. Her gray coat and skirt were torn and crumpled, and her hair hung down in wisps.

"Oh, poor Miss Price," cried Carey, running up, "whatever's the matter? Have you hurt yourself?"

Miss Price looked back with frightened eyes, and then she looked away.

"It's my ankle," she muttered.

Carey fell on her knees in the damp grass. Miss Price's ankle was indeed the strangest shape. "Oh, poor Miss Price," cried Carey again, and the tears came to her eyes. "It must hurt terribly."

"It does," said Miss Price.

"Run to the house, Charles," ordered Carey, "and tell them to ring up the doctor."

Then a strange look came over Miss Price's face, and her eyes opened wide as if with fright. "No, no," she stammered, gripping Carey's arm. "No, not that, just help me to get home."

The children looked at her, but they were not surprised. It did not even occur to them to wonder what Miss Price might be doing so early in the morning in their aunt's garden.

"Help me to get home," repeated Miss Price. "I can put one arm round your shoulders"—she looked at Carey—"and one round his. Then, perhaps, I can hop."

Paul watched seriously as Carey and Charles leaned toward Miss Price. Then he sighed. "And I'll carry this," he said obligingly, picking up a garden broom.

"We don't want that," Carey told him sharply. "Put it up against the tree."

"But it's Miss Price's."

"How do you mean—Miss Price's? It's the garden broom."

Paul looked indignant. "It isn't ours. It's hers. It's what she fell off. It's what she rides on."

Carey and Charles stood up, their faces red from stooping, and stared at Paul.

"What she rides on?"

"Yes. Don't you, Miss Price?"

Miss Price became paler than ever. She looked from one child to another. She opened her mouth and then she shut it again, as if no words would come.

"You're quite good at it, aren't you, Miss Price?" Paul went on encouragingly. "You weren't at first."

Then Miss Price began to cry. She pulled out her handkerchief and held it over her face. "Oh, dear," she said, "oh, dear! Now I suppose everybody knows."

Carey put her arms round Miss Price's neck. It was what you always did to people when they cried.

"It's all right, Miss Price. Nobody knows. Nobody knows at all. Paul didn't even tell us. It's quite all right. I think it's wonderful to ride on a broomstick."

"It's very difficult," said Miss Price, but she blew her nose.

They helped her to her feet. Carey felt puzzled and very excited, but she didn't like to ask any more. Slowly and painfully they made their way through the garden and down the lane that led to Miss Price's house. The rising sun glimmered through the hedgerows and turned the dust in the roadway to pale gold. Carey and Charles went very carefully, and Miss Price flapped between like a large gray bird with a broken wing.

Paul walked behind—with the broomstick.

2

More About Her

Afterward, on the way home, Carey and Charles tackled Paul.

"Paul, why didn't you tell us you'd seen Miss Price on a broomstick?"

"I dunno."

"But, Paul, you ought to have told us. We'd have liked to see it, too. It was very mean of you, Paul."

Paul did not reply.

"When did you see her?"

"In the night."

Paul looked stubborn. He felt as if he might be going to cry. Miss Price always passed so quickly. She would have been gone before he could call anyone, and they would have said at once, "Don't be silly, Paul." Besides, it had been his secret, his nightly joy. His bed was beside the window, and when the moon was full, it shone on his pillow and wakened him. It had been exciting to lie there, with his eyes fixed on the pale sky beyond the ragged blackness of the cedar boughs. Some nights he did not wake up. Other nights he woke up and she did not come. But he saw her often enough, and each time he saw her, she had learned to fly a little better. At first she had wobbled so, balanced sideways on the stick, that he wondered why she did not ride astride. She would grip the broomstick with one hand and try to hold her hat on with the other, and her feet, in their long shoes, looked so odd against the moonlit sky. Once she fell—and the broomstick came down quite slowly, like an umbrella blown inside out, with Miss Price clinging to the handle. Paul had watched her anxiously until she reached the ground. That time she landed safely.

Partly, he did not tell because he wanted to be proud of Miss Price. He did not want the others to see her until she was really good at it—until, perhaps, she could do tricks on a broomstick and look confident instead of scared. Once when she had lifted both hands in the air at the same time, Paul nearly clapped. He knew that was hard to do even on a bicycle.

"You see, Paul," Carey grumbled, "it was really very selfish; now Miss Price has hurt her ankle, she won't be flying again for ages. Charles and I may never have the chance of seeing her!"

Later, as they were solemnly eating lunch in the high, dark dining room, Aunt Beatrice startled them by saying suddenly, "Poor Miss Price!" They all looked up, as if she had read their secret thoughts, and were relieved when she went on calmly, "It seems she has fallen off her bicycle and sprained her ankle. So painful, poor soul. I must send her down some peaches."

Paul sat with his spoon halfway to his mouth, and his eyes moved round from Charles to Carey.

Carey cleared her throat. "Aunt Beatrice," she said, "could we take the peaches to Miss Price?"

"That's very thoughtful of you, Carey. I don't see why not, if you know where she lives."

Paul seemed about to burst into speech but was silenced by a kick from Charles; aggrievedly, he swallowed his last mouthful of rice pudding.

"Yes, Aunt Beatrice, we do know where she lives."

It was about four o'clock in the afternoon when the children knocked at Miss Price's neat front door. The path on which they stood was gaily bordered with flowers, and through the half-open windows of the sitting room, Miss Price's dimity curtains fluttered in the breeze. The door was opened by Agnes, a village girl who served Miss Price for a few hours daily.

As the children entered the little sitting room, for a moment they felt very shy. There lay Miss Price on the sofa, her bandaged foot raised up on pillows. She still looked pale, but now her hair was tidy and her white blouse spotlessly neat.

"What lovely peaches! Thank you, my dears, and thank your aunt. Very kind of her, I'm sure. Sit down, sit down."

The children sat down gingerly on the little spindly chairs.

"Agnes is making us some tea. You must stay and keep me company. Carey, can you open that card table?"

The children bustled round and helped to set the room for tea. A little table near Miss Price for the tea tray and a white cloth on the card table for the scones, the bread and butter, the quince jelly, and the ginger cake.

They enjoyed their tea, and when it was over, they helped Agnes to clear away. Then Miss Price showed Charles and Carey how to play backgammon and lent Paul a large book full of pictures called *Paradise Lost.* Paul liked the book very much. He liked the smell of it and the gilt-edged pages.

When they had finished the game of backgammon and it seemed that it must be nearly time to go home, Carey took her courage in both hands.

"Miss Price," she said hesitatingly, "if it isn't rude to ask—are you a witch?"

There was silence for a moment, and Carey could feel her heart beating. Paul looked up from his book.

Very carefully, Miss Price closed the backgammon board and laid it on the little table beside the sofa. She took up her knitting and unfolded it.

"Well," she said slowly, "I am and I'm not."

Paul sat back on his heels. "You mean, you are sort of," he suggested.

Miss Price threw him a glance. "I mean, Paul," she said quietly, "that I am studying to be a witch." She knitted a few stitches, pursing up her mouth.

"Oh, Miss Price!" cried Carey warmly. "How terribly clever of you!"

It was the best thing she could have said. Miss Price flushed, but she looked pleased.

"How did you first think of it, Miss Price?"

"Well, ever since I was a girl, I've had a bit of a gift for witchcraft, but somehow—what with piano lessons and looking after my mother—I never seemed to have the time to take it up seriously."

Paul was staring at Miss Price, as if to drink in

every detail of her appearance. "I don't think you're a wicked witch," he said at last.

Miss Price dropped her eyes unhappily. "I know, Paul," she admitted in a low voice. "You're quite right. I started too late in life. That's the whole trouble."

"Is being wicked the hardest part?" asked Carey.

"It is for me," Miss Price told her rather sadly. "But there are people who have a natural gift for it."

"Paul has," said Charles.

Paul came nearer and sat down on a chair. He was still staring at Miss Price, as if he longed to ask her something. After a minute, he found courage. "Could you just do a little bit of magic for us now?"

"Oh, Paul," exclaimed Carey, "don't worry Miss Price—she can't do magic with a sprained ankle."

"Yes, she could," protested Paul hotly. "She could do it lying down, couldn't you, Miss Price?"

"Well," said Miss Price, "I am a little tired, Paul. But I'll just do a little quick one, and then you must all go home. There you are!"

Carey and Charles looked around quickly, following the direction of Miss Price's eyes. Paul's chair was empty. Paul had gone—but where he had been sitting perched a little yellow frog.

Before Carey or Charles had time to exclaim,

Paul was back again, still staring expectantly at Miss Price.

"Oh," cried Carey, with a gasp, "that was wonderful, wonderful! How *did* you do it?"

She felt breathless and almost afraid. Magic—a spell—she had seen it with her own eyes.

"I didn't see anything," complained Paul.

Carey looked at him impatiently. "Oh, don't be silly, Paul. You turned into a frog. You must have felt it."

Paul's lips trembled. "I didn't feel anything," he said in a squeaky little voice. But nobody heard him. Carey was staring at Miss Price with shining eyes.

"Miss Price," she pointed out almost reproachfully, "you could have done that at the church concert, instead of singing."

Miss Price laid down her knitting. A strange look crept into her face, and she looked hard at Carey as if she were seeing her for the first time. Nervously, Carey drew back in her chair.

"Although you sing so nicely," she added quickly.

But Miss Price did not seem to hear. There was a wild light in her eyes, and her lips moved quietly, as if she were reciting. "There must be some way," she was saying slowly. "There—must—be—some—way . . ."

"Some way of what?" asked Charles after a moment's uncomfortable silence.

Miss Price smiled, showing her long yellow teeth.

"Of keeping your mouths shut," she rapped out.

Carey was shocked. This was far from ladylike. "Oh, Miss Price!" she exclaimed unhappily.

"Of keeping your mouths shut," repeated Miss Price slowly, smiling more unpleasantly than ever.

Paul made a little wriggling movement in his chair. "Now she's getting wicked," he whispered to Carey in a pleased voice.

Carey drew away from him as if she had not heard. She looked worried. "What do you mean, Miss Price? You mean we mustn't tell anyone that—" She hesitated.

"That you're a witch?" put in Paul.

But Miss Price was still staring, as if she neither heard nor saw. "In just a minute I'll think of something," she said, as if to herself. "In just a minute—"

Then Carey did something that Charles thought very brave. She got up from her chair and sat down beside Miss Price on the sofa.

"Listen, Miss Price," she said. "We did try to help you when you hurt your ankle. There isn't any need to use any kind of nasty magic on us. If you want to stop us telling, you could do it in a nice kind of way."

Miss Price looked at her. "How could I do it in a nice kind of way?" she asked, but she sounded more reasonable.

"Well," said Carey, "you could give us something—something magic—and if we told anyone about you, we'd have to forfeit it. You know, like a game. Directly we told, the thing would stop being magic."

"What sort of thing?" asked Miss Price, but as if the idea held possibilities.

Charles leaned forward. "Yes," he put in, "a ring or something that we could twist and a slave comes. And, if we told about you, the slave wouldn't come anymore. Couldn't you do that?"

Miss Price looked thoughtful. "I couldn't manage a slave," she said after a moment.

"Well, something like that."

Miss Price sat very quiet. She was thinking hard. "I know," she said after a while. Suddenly, she seemed quite nice and cheerful again. "There's something I've been wanting to try out. Mind you, I'm not sure that it will work. Has anybody got a ring on them?"

Alas, none of them had. Paul felt in his pockets,

just in case, but found nothing but the brass knob he had unscrewed from his bed that morning.

"Well, anything. A bracelet would do. It should be something you can twist."

But unfortunately, Carey could not produce a bracelet either. "I have one at home," she said, "but I only wear it on Sundays."

"You can twist this," cried Paul suddenly, holding out the bed-knob. "That's just what it does. It twists and it twists and it twists. I twisted it off," he added rather unnecessarily.

Miss Price took the bed-knob and held it thoughtfully between her clean, bony fingers.

"Let me see . . ." she said slowly. Then suddenly she looked up, as if surprised. "Paul, I believe this is the best thing you could have given me." Paul squirmed, pleased but bashful. "Now, I could do a wonderful spell with this—but I must think it out very carefully. Now, be quiet, children, and let me think—so that I can get this right." Her fingers closed gently round the shining brass. "This should be very good indeed. Now, quiet, please!"

The children sat like statues. Even Paul forgot to fidget. A bumblebee came in through the window and buzzed heavily about the room. Except for this, the silence was complete.

After what seemed a long while, Miss Price

opened her eyes. And then she sat up, blinking and smiling. "There you are, Paul," she said brightly, and handed him back the bed-knob.

He took it reverently. "Is it done?" he asked in an awestricken voice. It looked just the same to him.

"Yes, it's quite done," Miss Price told him. "And it's a very good spell indeed. This is something you'll enjoy. Only don't get yourselves into trouble."

Carey and Charles were looking enviously at Paul.

"What must we do with it?" asked Charles.

"Just take it home and screw it back on the bed. But don't screw it right up. Screw it about halfway."

"And then?"

"And then?" Miss Price smiled. "Twist it a little and wish—and the bed will take you to wherever you want to go!"

The children gazed unbelievingly at the gleaming ball in Paul's rather grubby fingers.

"Really?" asked Carey with a little gasp.

Miss Price was still smiling. She seemed very pleased with herself.

"Well, try it."

"Oh, Miss Price!" breathed Carey, still gazing at the knob. "*Thank* you."

"Don't thank me," said Miss Price, taking up her

knitting again. "Remember the conditions. One word about me and the spell is broken."

"Oh, Miss Price!" said Carey again. She was quite overcome.

"Well, now off you go. It's getting late. As I say, don't get yourselves into trouble and don't go gallivanting around all night. There should be moderation in all things—even in magic."

3

A False Start

At about ten o'clock next morning, the children were back again. Their faces were serious and their manner was uncertain.

"Could I—" said Carey to the cheerful Agnes, "could we see Miss Price?" She gave a little swallow, as if she felt nervous.

"Miss Price is engaged at the moment," replied Agnes. "Is there a message?"

"Well—" Carey hesitated. How much did Agnes know? She looked around at the others. Charles stepped forward.

"Could you just tell her," he said, "that it didn't work?"

"It didn't work?" repeated Agnes.

"Yes. Just say, 'It didn't work.'"

"It didn't work," repeated Agnes to herself, as if memorizing the message. She disappeared down the passage, leaving the front door open. They heard her knock. Then, after a minute, Agnes returned.

"Miss Price says will you step in."

They were shown once more into the sitting room. Each chose a chair and sat on the edge of it.

"I bet she'll be angry," whispered Paul, breaking the silence.

"Shush," said Carey. She looked a little pale.

Suddenly the door opened and Miss Price limped in. Her foot was bandaged, and she wore a carpet slipper, but she was able to walk without a stick. She looked round from face to face. "It didn't work?" she said slowly.

"No," replied Carey, clasping her hands together in her lap.

Miss Price sat down in the center of the sofa. They all stared at each other in silence.

"Are you sure you did it right?"

"Yes, just what you said. We half screwed it on, then turned it a little and wished."

"And what happened?"

"Nothing," said Carey. Paul's eyes, round with accusation, were fixed on Miss Price's face.

"I can't understand it," said Miss Price after a moment. She thought awhile. "Have you got it with you?" she asked.

Yes, Carey had it, in a checked sponge bag. Miss

Price drew out the golden ball and gazed at it non-plussed.

"Didn't the bed move at *all*?"

"Only by Paul bouncing on it."

"It's rusty here at the bottom," said Miss Price.

"It was always like that," Carey told her.

"Well, I don't know." Miss Price stood up, gingerly putting her strained foot to the floor. "I'll take it along and test it."

She made a move toward the door.

"Could we watch you?"

Miss Price turned back slowly. The circle of eager eyes seemed to hold her. They saw her hesitate. "Please, Miss Price!" urged Carey.

"No one has seen my workroom," said Miss Price. "Not even Agnes."

Carey was going to say, "But we're in the secret," but she thought better of it and kept quite quiet. Their longing eyes spoke for all of them.

"Well, I'll just send Agnes off for the groceries and then I'll see."

She went out. And it seemed an eternity before she called them. Eagerly they ran out into the passage. Miss Price was putting on a white overall. In her hand was a key. They followed her down two or three steps into a short dark passage. They heard the key turn in a well-oiled lock. Miss Price went in first, then stood aside.

"Quietly," she said, beckoning them in. "And careful what you touch."

The room must at one time have been a larder. There were marble slabs and wooden shelves above the slabs. The first thing Carey noticed were the glass jars, each with its typewritten label. Miss Price, a spot of proud pink in each cheek, ran a hand along the rows.

"Toads, hares' feet, bats' wings—oh, dear!" She picked up an empty jar to which a few damp balls still clung. "I'm out of newts' eyes!" She peered into the jar before she stood it back upon the shelf; then, taking up a pencil, she made a note on a memo pad that hung upon the wall. "They're almost impossible to get nowadays," she said with a sigh. "But we mustn't grumble. This is my little filing cabinet where I record results, successful—and unsuccessful, too, I'm afraid. My notebooks..."

Carey, leaning forward, saw these were stout exercise books, neatly labeled.

"Spells...Charms...Incantations," she read aloud.

"And I don't suppose any of you know," said Miss Price brightly, "the difference between a spell and a charm."

"I thought they were the same thing," said Charles.

"A-ha," replied Miss Price darkly, but her face was alight with hidden knowledge. "I only wish a spell *were* as easy as a charm."

She lifted a spotless piece of butter muslin, and the children peered, not without a shudder, at what appeared to be a greenish slab of meat. It lay symmetrically in a gleaming porcelain dish and smelled faintly of chemicals.

"What is it?" asked Carey.

Miss Price eyed the dish dubiously. "It's poisoned dragon's liver," she said uncertainly.

"Oh," said Carey politely.

Paul pushed up close. "Did you poison the dragon, Miss Price? Or just the liver?" he added.

"Well," admitted the truthful Miss Price, "as a matter of fact, it came ready prepared. It's part of the equipment."

"It all looks very hygienic," ventured Carey timidly.

"My dear Carey," said Miss Price reprovingly, "we have progressed a *little* since the Middle Ages. Method and prophylactics have revolutionized modern witchcraft."

Carey felt Miss Price was quoting from a book,

and she longed to know a little more. "Could I just see Lesson I?" she asked.

Miss Price glanced quickly at a pile of folders on an upper shelf, and then she shook her head. "I'm sorry, Carey. This course is absolutely confidential. 'Any infringement of this regulation,'" she quoted, "'entails a fine of not less than two hundred pounds and condemns the offender to chronic, progressively recurring, attacks of Cosmick Creepus.'"

Paul looked pensive. "It's cheaper to spit in a bus," he announced, after some seconds of silent thought.

Gradually, the children discovered other treasures: a chart on which the signs of the zodiac were nicely touched up by Miss Price in watercolor; a sheep's skull; a chocolate box full of dried mice; herbs in bunches; a pot of growing hemlock and one of witch's bane; a small stuffed alligator, which hung by two wires from the ceiling.

"What are alligators used for, Miss Price?" asked Paul.

Again Miss Price's long training in truthfulness overcame her longing to impress. "Nothing much," she said. "They're out of date now. I like to have it there for the look of it."

"It does look nice," Paul agreed rather enviously. He stuck his hands in his pockets. "I had a dead hen once," he added carelessly.

But Miss Price did not hear him. She was arranging three hazel twigs on a shelf in the form of a triangle. In the center of this, she set the bed-knob.

"Now pass me that red notebook, just by your hand, Carey."

"The one marked 'Spells, Elementary'?"

"No, dear. The one marked 'Spells, Advanced, Various.' Really, Carey," Miss Price exclaimed, as Carey passed her a book, "can't you read? This is 'Six Easy Curses for Beginners'..."

"Oh, I'm sorry," cried Carey quickly, and looked again. "This is it, I think."

Miss Price took the book. She put on her spectacles and spent some time gazing at the open page. Picking up a pencil, she scribbled a few figures on a piece of shelf paper. She stared at these, and then she rubbed them out with the other end of the pencil.

"Miss Price—" began Paul.

"Don't interrupt me," murmured Miss Price. "Hellebore, henbane, aconite... glowworm fire and firefly light... Better pull down the shades, Carey."

"The shades, Miss Price?"

"Yes, over the window. Or we shan't be able to see this experiment."

Carey pulled down the shades and adjusted them. As the room became dark, Miss Price exclaimed, "Now, isn't that pretty!" She sounded surprised and delighted. The children crowded round her and saw

that the bed-knob glowed with a gentle light—pale as early dawn. As they watched, Miss Price twisted the knob a little, and the pale light turned to rose.

"There, you see!" Miss Price said triumphantly. "What's wrong with that, I'd like to know? Pull up the blinds again, Carey."

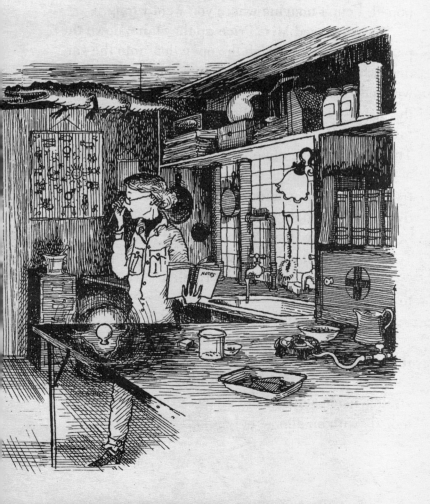

Carey rolled up the blinds and hooked the oil-cloth on its little hook. Miss Price slipped an elastic band round the three hazel twigs and tidied up the notebooks.

"Come along," she said cheerfully, opening the door. "The spell works perfectly. Better than I hoped. I can't imagine where you went wrong."

They followed Miss Price up the stairs, down the passage, and out through the open door into the garden, where the air was sweet with the smell of sun-warmed earth. Butterflies balanced precariously on the spears of lavender, and bumblebees hung in the foxglove bells. A milkman's cart stopped at the gate. There was a clang of bottles.

"Thank you ever so much," said Carey. "We'll try it again this evening. I did just what you said. I didn't screw it tight at all. I—"

"You?" said Miss Price. "You did it, Carey?"

"Yes. I did it myself. I was very careful. I—"

"But, Carey," said Miss Price, "I gave the spell to Paul."

"You mean Paul should've—?"

"Of course. Paul should have done it. No wonder it didn't work."

Slowly, wonderingly, a grin of ecstasy began to stretch itself across Paul's face. His eyes gleamed moistly with an almost holy joy.

Carey and Charles looked at him as though they had never seen him before.

"Well?" said Miss Price rather sharply.

Charles found his voice. "He's sort of young," he pointed out, "for so much responsibility."

But Miss Price was firm. "The younger the better, as I know to my cost. Now run along, children." She turned away, but almost immediately she turned back again, lowering her voice. "Oh, by the way, I meant to tell you something else. You know I said the spell was better than I hoped. Well, if you twist it one way, the bed will take you where you want, in the present. Twist it the other way and the bed will take you back into the past."

"Oh, Miss Price!" exclaimed Carey.

"What about the future?" asked Charles.

Miss Price looked at him as the bus conductor looks when you ask for a ticket to a place off the bus route. Charles blushed and churned up the gravel path with the toe of his shoe.

"Now, remember what I said," went on Miss Price. "Have a good time, keep to the rules, and *allow for the bed.*"

She turned to the milkman, who had been waiting patiently by the step. "Half a pint, please, Mr. Bisselthwaite, and my butter."

4

The Preliminary Canter

It was hard to get through the rest of the day, but evening came at last; by the time it was Paul's bedtime, anticipation had made them tired and excitement had grown stale.

"Look here, Paul," said Carey suddenly, as Paul was brushing his teeth. "You wouldn't go and do it by yourself. You'll lie still till Charles and I come to bed, won't you?"

Paul looked at her over the slowly revolving brush.

"If you went off on that bed by yourself," continued Carey, "and it went wrong, no one could save you. You might get stuck in the past or anything."

Paul spat into the hole in the basin. He watched the hole, and then, carefully, he spat again. He felt aggrieved; from the moment he had screwed on the bed-knob, after getting back from Miss Price's, Carey and Charles had not let him out of their sight for an instant. It was his bed after all, and, what was more, his bed-knob. They might have let him have a trial run, just to the bottom of the garden, say, and back. He hadn't wanted to go far, but he had wanted to know if it really worked.

"You see, Paul," went on Carey, "suppose Elizabeth came upstairs with your milk, and the bed was gone. What then? We've got to be very careful. It may seem deceitful, but we *did* promise Miss Price. You can't go tearing about on the bed in broad daylight, and things like that."

Paul rinsed his mouth and swallowed the water, as was his custom.

"Do you see, Paul? We've got to wait until they're all in bed. Come here, and I'll comb your hair while it's wet."

They followed him into his bedroom. They sat on the bed. They all looked at the bed-knob, just above Paul's right ear; it looked just like the other three.

"I bet it doesn't work," said Charles. "I bet you anything."

"Shush," said Carey, as Elizabeth came in with their milk on a tray.

"Don't spill on the sheet, now," she said, panting, "and bring the tray down, Miss Carey, please; it's my evening out."

"Your evening out?" repeated Carey. She began to smile.

"Nothing funny in that, I hope," said Elizabeth tartly. "I've earned it. And no tricks, now; your aunt's not herself. She's gone to bed."

"Gone to bed?" echoed Carey again. She caught back the rest of her smile just in time. Elizabeth looked at her curiously.

"No tricks, now," she repeated. "There's something funny about you children. Butter wouldn't melt in your mouths, but I'm not so sure."

They heard her sigh on the landing. They heard her turn the corner. Then they kicked off their slippers and danced. Noiselessly, tensely, breathlessly, they gyrated and whirled and leaped; then, panting, they fell onto Paul's bed.

"Where shall we go?" whispered Carey, her eyes shining.

"Let's try a South Sea island," said Charles.

Paul bit deeply into his bread. His cheeks bulged and his jaws moved slowly. He was the calmest of the three.

"The Rocky Mountains," suggested Carey.

"The South Pole," said Charles.

"The Pyramids."

"Tibet."

"The moon."

"Where would you like to go, Paul?" asked Carey suddenly. Happiness had made her unselfish.

Paul swallowed his mouthful of bread and butter. "I'd like to go to the Natural History Museum."

"Oh, Paul," said Carey. "Not that kind of place. You can go there any time."

"I'd like to see the Big Flea in the Natural History Museum," said Paul. He remembered how Carey and Charles had gone with an uncle, without him, when he, Paul, had been in bed with a cold.

"It was only a model. Think of another place, Paul. You can have first turn, as it's your bed. But somewhere nice."

"I'd like to go to London," said Paul.

"But you can go to London almost anytime," Charles reminded him.

"I'd like to go to London to see my mother."

"Don't say 'my mother.' She's our mother, too."

"I'd like to see her," repeated Paul simply.

"Well, we'd like to see her," admitted Carey. "But she'd be kind of surprised."

"I'd like to see my mother." Paul's lips began to tremble, and his eyes filled with tears. Carey looked worried.

"Paul," she tried to explain, "when you get a thing as magic as this, you don't make that kind of wish, like seeing your mother and going to museums and things; you wish for something absolutely extraordinary. Don't you see, Paul? Try again."

Paul's face turned crimson, and the tears rolled out of his eyes and down his cheeks.

"I'd like to see my mother, or the Big Flea." He was trying not to sob aloud. He closed his lips, and his chest heaved up and down.

"Oh, dear," said Carey desperately. She stared down at her shoes.

"Let him have his turn," Charles suggested in a patient voice. "We can go somewhere else afterward."

"But don't you see—" began Carey. "Oh, all right," she added. "Come on. Get on the bed, Charles." She began to feel excited again.

"Let's all hold on to the rails. Better tuck in that bit of blanket. Now, Paul, take hold of the knob—gently. Here, I'll blow your nose. Now, are you ready?"

Paul knelt up, facing the head of the bed and the wall. He had his hand on the knob. "What shall I say?"

"Say Mother's address. Say, 'I wish to be at No. 38 Markham Square,' and twist."

"I wish to be—" Paul's voice sounded thick. He cleared his throat.

"At No. 38," prompted Carey.

"At No. 38."

"Markham Square."

"Markham Square."

Nothing happened. There was an awful moment of suspense, then Carey added quickly, "S.W.3."

"S.W.3," repeated Paul.

It was horrible. It was a swooshing rush, as if the world had changed into a cinema film run too quickly. A jumble that was almost fields, almost trees, almost streets, almost houses, but nothing long enough. The bed rocked. They clung to the railings. The bed-clothes whipped round Carey and Charles, who clung to the foot, blinding them, choking them. A great seasick lurch. Then bang...bump...clang...and a sliding scrape.

They had arrived.

They felt shaken and breathless. Slowly Carey unwound a blanket from her neck and head. Her mouth was full of fluff. The eiderdown was blown tight round Charles and hung through the brass rails of the bed. Paul was still kneeling on the pillow. His face was scarlet and his hair was blown upright.

"Gosh," said Charles after a moment. He looked about him. They were indeed in Markham Square. The bed had come to rest neatly alongside the pave-ment, nearly touching the curb. There was No. 38 with its black front door, its checkered steps, and the area railing. Charles felt extraordinarily conspicuous. The bed was so very much a bed and the street so very much a street, and there was Paul crossing the pavement in his bare feet to ring the front doorbell. Paul, in his pajamas and with such untidy hair, standing on Mother's front steps in broad daylight—a warm, rich evening light, but nonetheless broad daylight.

Charles prayed for the door to open quickly. He was by nature extremely retiring.

A red bus rolled by at the end of the square. For the moment, the pavement was empty.

"Ring again," he cried fervently. Paul rang again.

They heard the echo of the bell in the basement, a polite, regretful, empty sound. The dark windows stared blankly.

"There's no one at home," said Carey when they had waited a minute or two longer. She uncurled her legs. "Mother must have gone out to dinner," she announced, standing up. "Well, we'll have to wait. Let's tidy the bed."

As they made the bed, drawing up the blankets, turning back the sheets, plumping up the pillows, Charles marveled at Carey's and Paul's lack of concern. Didn't they think it odd, he wondered, to be making a bed there in a London street? He glanced longingly toward the area steps. "Shall we try the back door?" he suggested—anything to be away from the bed and down below the level of the pavement. He couldn't go far because he hadn't any shoes on.

They crept down the area steps. They rattled and pulled at the tradesmen's door. It was locked. They peered in at the kitchen window. A cup and saucer lay on the drainboard; the rest of the kitchen was curiously tidy and deathly still. The window was fastened. Even breaking it would have done no good. It was barred against burglars.

"We must just sit on the bed and wait," sighed Carey.

"Not on the bed," said Charles hastily. "Let's stay down here, where no one can see us," he added.

They all squeezed together on the bottom step, facing the dustbin. The area smelled of wet tea leaves, and the step was cold.

"I don't call this much of an adventure," said Charles.

"Nor do I," agreed Carey. "It was Paul's idea."

It grew darker. Looking upward, they saw that the light was draining quickly from the street above. There was mist in the air.

They began to hear passersby. The footsteps

always paused at No. 38, and the children, listening, realized how much grown-ups think alike. They nearly all said, with deep surprise, "How funny! A bed!" or "A bed! How funny!" Always they heard the word "Bed—bed, bed, bed" and footsteps. Once Charles spoke for them. As he heard the footsteps pause, he said aloud, "How funny, a bed!" It was almost dark then, and a form peered down at them over the area railings. "Some children," muttered a

voice, as if explaining to a second person. As the footsteps died away, Charles called after them, "And a bed."

"Don't, Charles, it's rude. You'll get us into trouble."

It became quite dark, a darkness laced with mist.

"River fog," said Charles, "and if you ask me, I think Mother's gone away for the weekend."

Paul was already asleep against Carey's shoulder. Carey had a sudden brain wave.

"I know!" she exclaimed. "Let's get into the bed! It's quite dark now. If it's foggy enough, no one will see us."

They went up the steps again and crossed the pavement. Ah! It was good to crawl under the blankets and to pull up the eiderdown. Above them the sky looked grayish between the steep black roofs. The stars had disappeared.

"I honestly don't call this much of an adventure," whispered Charles.

"I know," Carey replied. "But it's the first time. We'll get better at it."

Between them, Paul breathed deeply, exuding a pleasant warmth.

Carey must have been asleep for some time when the shock came. At first, shaken out of a dream, she

lay quite still. Damp darkness...her legs felt pin-
ioned. Where was she? Then she remembered.

"Please!" she cried, with an agonized squeak.
The fog had deepened. She could see nothing.

There was a hoarse gasp. "Well, I'll be——"

"Please," cried Carey again, interrupting. "*Please*
get off my foot."

A light flashed on, a terrifying dazzling circle;
shining straight in their eyes as it did, it felt like a
searchlight.

The gruff voice said again, "Well, I'll be blowed—
kids!"

The weight lifted itself, and thankfully Carey
curled back her legs, blinking at the glare. She
knew suddenly, without being able to see a thing,
that behind that light was a policeman. She felt a
policeman, large and tall and fat and creaking.

He switched off his flashlight. "Kids!" he said
again in a surprised voice. Then he became stern.
"Can't 'ave this, you know." He breathed heavily.
"Can't 'ave beds, like this, in the street. Danger to
the public. Caught me on the shin, this bed did. A
street's no place for beds. Where's your mother?"

"I don't know," said Carey in a low voice.

"Speak up," said the policeman. "What's your
name?"

"Carey Wilson."

On went the light again and out came a note-book. Again the policeman sat down. The bed creaked, but Carey's toes were out of reach.

"Address?"

Charles sat up sleepily. "What?" he said.

Carey had a sudden vision of Aunt Beatrice's face, the tight lips, the pink-rimmed eyes. She thought of her mother, worried, upset. Letters, policemen, complaints, fines, prison.

"Look," said Carey, "I'm terribly sorry we hurt your shin. If you just move, we'll take the bed away, and then you won't be troubled anymore. We'll take it right away. Really."

"This 'ere's an iron bed," said the policeman. "This 'ere bed's good and heavy."

"We can take it," urged Carey. "We brought it here. We have a way of taking it."

"I don't see no way of taking this bed any-where—not in this fog."

"If you'd just move a moment," said Carey, "we'll show you."

"Not so fast, miss." The policeman was getting into his stride. "I'm not moving anywhere, just at present. Where did you bring this 'ere bed *from*?"

Carey hesitated. Trouble—that was what they were heading for. She thought again of Aunt Beatrice. And of Miss Price—oh, Miss Price, that was almost the worst of all; to tell about Miss Price would be the end of everything—yet no good ever came of lying.

"Well," said Carey, trying to think quickly.

"We brought it from my room," put in Paul suddenly.

"Oh," said the policeman heavily. He had adopted a slightly sarcastic tone to hide his bewilderment. "And where might your room be?"

"Next to Carey's," said Paul. "At the end of the passage."

The policeman, who had switched off his light, switched it on again right into Paul's eyes. Carey and Charles, who up to that moment had thought little or nothing of Paul's looks, suddenly realized that he had a face like an angel. Two little wings could have been tied to his back and they would not have looked out of place. Even a halo would have suited Paul.

The policeman switched out his light. "Poor little shaver," he muttered, "dragging 'im round London at this time o' night."

This was more than Carey could stand. "Why," she cried indignantly, "it's all his fault. It was all his idea—"

"Now, now," said the policeman. "That's enough.

What I want to know is, where did you get this 'ere bed? What part o' London, to be exact?"

"It didn't come from London at all," said Charles.

"Then *where* did it come from?" thundered the policeman.

"From Bedfordshire," said Carey.

The policeman stood up. Carey heard him catch his breath angrily.

"Joke, eh?"

"Not at all," said Carey.

"You mean to tell me you brought this 'ere bed all the way up from Bedfordshire?"

"Yes," said Carey.

The policeman sighed. Carey felt him trying to be patient. "By train?"

"No," said Carey.

"Then how, may I ask?"

"Well—" said Carey. She thought again of Miss Price. "Well, we can't really tell you."

"You tell me how you brought this bed up from Bedfordshire or you come along with me to the police station—where you're coming anyway," he added.

"All right," said Carey, feeling the tears sting into her eyes. "I'll tell you. If you want to know, we brought it up by magic."

There was a silence. A terrific silence. Carey

wondered if the policeman was going to hit her with his truncheon, but when at last he spoke, he spoke very quietly. "Oh, you did, did you? By magic. Now I'll tell you something. You've 'eard of the law, 'aven't you? Well, the law is just and, in a manner of speaking, the law is kind, but there's one thing the law can't be—" He took a deep breath. "The law can't be made fun of. Now, all three of you, get out of that there bed and come along with me to the station!"

With a sinking heart Carey drew her legs from under the blankets.

"I haven't any shoes on," said Charles.

There was no reply. The policeman seemed drawn away from them in spirit, wrapped in lofty silence.

"Nor has Paul," pointed out Carey. "You'll have to carry him," she added.

5

The Police Station

It was not a long walk, but it was a trying one for Charles in his stocking feet. Never before had he realized quite how many different kinds of surface go to make a London street. Paul rode majestically in the policeman's arms, sharing the policeman's vast aloofness. Carey walked in dark depression. Every step they took away from the bed decreased their chances of escape. Prison! "Oh," she thought in desperation, "why didn't I tell Paul to wish the bed away with us, policeman and all?" But that might have been even more complicated; arriving back at Aunt Beatrice's with a policeman; trying to smuggle a policeman out of Paul's bedroom, to smuggle a policeman out of the house...and he wasn't at all the kind of policeman who would lend himself to being smuggled anywhere. There was, Carey realized unhappily, practically no reliable method of getting rid of unwanted policemen. No, bad as it was, this possibly was the lesser of the two evils.

They were in the police station almost before they knew it. There was a long counter, a green-shaded light, and a gray-haired policeman without a hat. He had a tired, thin face, a soldier's face. Carey felt herself trembling.

"Well, Sergeant?" said the gray-haired officer wearily. "I thought we were through for tonight."

"Well, sir, these 'ere children, sir. Thought I'd better bring 'em along. Out in the street, with a bed, sir. Obstructing traffic—public nuisance, as it were."

The inspector was reaching for his cap, which hung on a peg.

"Well, take their names and addresses and get hold of the parents." He paused and turned slowly. "Out in the street with a what?"

"With a bed, sir."

"A *bed*!"

"Yes, sir, an iron bed like, with brass knobs on."

The inspector looked wonderingly at Carey. Suddenly Carey knew she liked his face. She liked the screwed-up look of his eyes and the tired lines of his mouth. She wished terribly that she had not been brought before him as a criminal. He looked at all three of them for a moment longer, then he addressed the sergeant.

"Where is the bed now?"

"There in the street, sir. Markham Square."

"Better send the van to collect the bed." He sighed. "And hand these children over to Mrs. Watkins till you get hold of the parents. I'm dead beat, Sergeant. Court at nine-thirty, don't forget. I'll need you and Sergeant Coles."

"Yes, sir. Good night, sir."

As the inspector passed, on his way to the door, he glanced again at the children. "He would have talked to us," Carey thought, "if he hadn't been so tired." She felt very frightened. If only someone had scolded them, she would have felt less frightened. She felt as if something bigger than a person had got hold of them, something enormous, something of which the policemen themselves stood in awe. She guessed it was the "law"—the law that "could not be made fun of."

The sergeant was speaking into a telephone, which hung from a bracket on the wall.

"Yes, three of 'em ... No—just overnight ... No, 'e's gone off. Dead beat, 'e was ... Cup o' tea? Not if you got it made, I wouldn't ... Righty oh."

He brought out his notebook and wrote down

their mother's address. "Why," he said, after some minutes of silent and ponderous calculation. "You was right by your own 'ouse."

"Mother's away," said Carey quickly, hoping to stop him ringing up.

"Did you say you brought the bed up from Bedfordshire?"

"We did," said Carey. "The house is locked up."

The policeman was busy writing. "Right by your own 'ouse," he murmured. "That's different."

"Well," he said, closing his notebook. "Come along with me for the time being."

He took the children down a passage, out of a back door into a pitch-dark courtyard. "Mind where you tread," he told them.

Paul took Carey's hand. "Are we going to prison?" he whispered.

"I don't know," Carey whispered back. "I think so."

"How many years," asked Paul, "will they keep us in prison?"

"I don't know," said Carey, "not many."

"Come on," said the sergeant. They felt he was holding a door open. They squeezed past his stomach into another passage. They were indoors again. The sergeant switched on a light. "Mrs. Watkins," he called.

Mrs. Watkins was a bustling kind of woman, a cross—Carey thought—between a cloakroom attendant and a nurse. She wore a white apron and a red woolen cardigan over it. She took them into a room in which there was a bed—like a hospital bed, thought Carey—two imitation-leather armchairs, a table, and an aspidistra in a pot. She bustled Paul onto the bed and covered him with a blanket. Then she turned to Charles and Carey. "Cocoa or tea?" she asked them.

Carey hesitated. "Whichever's easiest for you," she said politely.

"The sergeant's having tea."

"Well, tea if you've got it made," said Carey timidly. "Thank you very much," she added.

Mrs. Watkins stared at Carey for a minute. "Lost, are you?" she asked curiously.

Carey, sitting on the edge of the imitation-leather armchair, smiled uneasily. "Not exactly."

"Up to mischief?" asked Mrs. Watkins.

Carey blushed, and tears came into her eyes. "Not exactly," she stammered.

"Well," said Mrs. Watkins kindly, "you sit there quiet and be good children and you'll have a nice cup o' tea."

"Thank you," murmured Carey indistinctly.

As the door closed behind Mrs. Watkins and

the key turned in the lock, Carey burst into tears. Charles stared at her miserably, and Paul, sitting up in bed with interest, asked, "What are you crying for, Carey?"

"This is all so awful," wept Carey, trying at the same time to stanch her tears with her handkerchief.

"I don't think it's so awful," said Paul. "I like this prison."

Charles glared at him. "Only because you're going to have a cup of tea, and you know you're not allowed tea at home."

"No," said Paul rather vaguely, "I like prisons like this."

"Well, it isn't even a prison. It's a police station."

"Oh," said Paul. He gazed about the room, but a little less happily.

"Paul," said Carey some time later, when they had drunk their tea and Mrs. Watkins had left them alone again, "I told you this was a stupid kind of wish. I tried to warn you. It would have been better to go back into the Middle Ages or anything than this. This is worse than anything that has ever happened to us. We've lost the bed. The policeman will ring up Mother. Mother will be terribly worried. The law may get her too. Aunt Beatrice will know. They'll make us explain everything. Miss Price will get into trouble. We shall have broken our promise. It will be the end of the magic bed-knob. And nobody will ever trust us again . . ."

Paul looked grave.

"Do you see, Paul?" Carey's voice sounded as if she were going to cry again. "And it's Charles and me who'll get the blame. They'll say we led you into it, that we're old enough to know better. Do you understand?"

Paul brightened perceptibly. "Yes," he said.

"We're locked in here. And there isn't anything we can do."

She broke off. Suddenly outside in the courtyard there was a screech of brakes. They heard the running engine of a car, and voices shouting.

"They're bringing someone else in!" exclaimed Paul excitedly.

Charles went up to the window, but he dared not disturb the blind. "They'll see us," he said.

"I know what," cried Carey. "Switch out this light!"

Charles switched off the light by the door. Then, in the darkness, he tugged a corner of the blind. It flew up with a rattle. A pinkish light, faint but clear, shone inward on the room.

"It's dawn," said Charles wonderingly. "Morning.

We've been away all night." He stared down into the
courtyard.

    "I say, Carey—"

    "What?"

"They're not bringing anyone in. It's—" He paused excitedly. "Carey, it's the bed!"

Carey leaped out of her chair, and Paul threw off the blanket. They raced to the window. They watched, in that dim early light, two policemen lift the bed from the van. They heard the legs scrape as it was dragged across the cobblestones. They saw the policemen push it up against the wall. Then both men stood, rubbing the strain out of their hands and staring at the bed. They laughed. "I could do with a nap meself," said one as they walked away indoors. Then the courtyard became silent.

"If we could get to it—" breathed Charles.

"If—" said Carey.

The pale light shone softly on their faces as, longingly, they stared out through the bars.

6

Magic in the Courtyard

At about nine o'clock next morning, the sergeant and the inspector faced each other across the inspector's desk. The sergeant was standing. His hat was in his hand and his face was very red.

"...and that's all I know, sir," the sergeant was saying.

"But how did they get away?" asked the inspector. "I'm afraid I don't follow you, Sergeant. How did they get into the yard to start with?"

"Well, Mrs. Watkins took 'em down, sir, to see my garden."

"To see your garden?" repeated the inspector in a surprised voice.

"Them dahlias, sir, in pots, at the end of the yard, sir. Mrs. Watkins calls 'em my garden. I got some sweet peas, sir, too—coming up nicely, the sweet peas are."

"I didn't know you were a horticulturist, Sergeant." The inspector spoke rather coldly. "And then?"

"Mrs. Watkins, she quite took to those kids, sir. She thought they'd like to see the bird, sir, too."

"The bird?"

"I got a canary down there, sir. I was putting it out, like, in the sun, early this morning."

"Have you got anything else down there in the yard?"

The sergeant shuffled his feet.

"Well, sir, only the silkworms."

The inspector glanced out of the window, pursing up his mouth in a rather peculiar way as if he were trying to keep it still.

"And you left the children alone in the yard?" he asked sternly.

"Well, sir, the gate was locked, sir. Roberts was on duty outside. I'd just slipped in the passage to sip a cup o' tea Mrs. Watkins 'ad there waiting."

"Well, go on. How long were you sipping this tea?"

"No time at all, sir. I just took the cup like from Mrs. Watkins, put in a bit of sugar, stirred it, and came right out to the door—"

"And then—?"

"Well, I couldn't see the children. I thought at first they was round be'ind the pillars." The sergeant wiped his face with his handkerchief. "But no," he added."

"They'd gone."

"Yes, sir, they'd gone."

"And the bed, too."

"Yes, sir, and the bed, too. We searched the premises. The yard gate was still padlocked. Roberts said he 'adn't seen nothing."

The inspector stared at his fingernails. "Very peculiar. Mrs. Watkins bears out your story?"

"Yes, sir."

"Mrs. Watkins took to them, you say?"

"Yes, sir. They were nice kids, sir, well brought up. I got sort of sore with 'em last night. 'Urt my leg on that there bed of theirs. But they weren't bad, not at 'eart they weren't."

The inspector leaned back in his chair. "You took to them yourself, in fact?"

"Not last night I didn't. But this morning—well, sir, they were so pleased like to see my little bird."

"You regretted perhaps," said the inspector slowly, fixing the sergeant with his eye, "having brought them in at all."

The sergeant stared back at the inspector. His eyes became very round and blue in his red face. He opened his mouth with a gasp. "You think I went and let them out, sir?" Then his fat face became stern and dignified. He swallowed. "I wouldn't do a thing like that. I know my duty, sir." He looked hurt and stared at a spot on the wall above the inspector's head.

The inspector smiled. "I'm sorry, Sergeant, if I've misjudged you. But you've told me a very tall story, you know. If the front gate is locked, there's absolutely no way out of the yard."

"I know, sir."

"And there's this business of the bed . . ."

"Yes, sir," said the sergeant.

"These children couldn't be considered in any way as delinquents. They were just having some prank, isn't that so?"

"Yes, sir." Suddenly a curious, half-shy look came into the sergeant's eyes. He twisted his hat round in his hands. He looked at the inspector as if he hardly dared put his thought into words.

"Something just occurred to me, sir." The sergeant was blushing.

"Well?"

"The little girl, when I asked 'er 'ow she brought the bed up from Bedfordshire . . ."

"Yes?"

The sergeant dropped his voice. "She said she brought it up by magic."

For a moment the inspector did not speak; then, "Really, Sergeant—" he said weakly.

The sergeant's blush became deeper. "I know, sir," he said humbly.

"Really, Sergeant," went on the inspector, standing up and beginning to gather together the papers he would need in court. "You're a grown man, now. You must curb these fancies."

7

Carey Has an Idea

It was with a feeling of great relief that the children found themselves back again in Paul's bedroom. Carey and Charles barely had time to wash themselves and to dress Paul before Elizabeth sounded the gong for breakfast. Paul nearly fell asleep over his porridge, and Carey and Charles felt guilty when, later on, Elizabeth thanked them for having made the beds they hadn't slept in. Their adventure did not seem like a dream, but it seemed as if they had been away for much longer than one night, and all of them felt very sleepy.

"Let's go down and see Miss Price this morning," suggested Carey, "and this afternoon let's go up to the hayloft and sleep till teatime."

They found Miss Price kneeling at her flower border, planting. She wore a large straw hat and a canvas apron with pockets. It was a lovely day, and the scented garden lay a-dream in the blazing warmth of the sun.

"Well," said Miss Price, sitting back and staring anxiously at their flushed, perspiring faces, "did it work?"

"Yes," said Carey. "It worked like magic—I mean, like a charm—I mean . . . Oh, Miss Price, it *did* work." She flung herself down on the grass beside Miss Price.

"Did you enjoy yourselves?" asked Miss Price rather anxiously. "Paul looks as though he can hardly keep his eyes open."

Carey pulled up a little tuft of the sweet-smelling lawn.

"Well, we didn't exactly *enjoy* ourselves," she admitted, and tried to push the tuft back again.

"You didn't!" exclaimed Miss Price. She looked worried.

Then out came the whole story. The children often interrupted each other, and sometimes they spoke in chorus, but gradually Miss Price pieced the pattern together. She became graver and graver as they described their adventures with the law and looked aghast when she heard they had actually been taken to the police station. She looked sad when Charles told her how the prison van had brought the bed into the yard and how they had stared at it through the barred window, but she brightened considerably when they got to the bit about the sergeant's garden. Carey copied Mrs. Watkins's voice saying, "Well, pop down and look at the bird, then, but don't you touch them dahlias." They didn't have to describe the rest. Miss Price knew too well what would happen once they were in reach of the bed. "Did anyone see you go?" she asked.

"No," said Carey, "that's when the sergeant went inside for his cup of tea."

"Did the bed go at once?"

"Yes, like a flash. The second that Paul wished. We'd hardly got on it."

"Well," said Miss Price thoughtfully, "let's hope they *don't* ring up your mother."

"Mother would say it couldn't have been us," pointed out Charles. "She'd know we couldn't have been in London."

"That's true, Charles," agreed Carey. "And Aunt Beatrice would say at once that we were here. We couldn't have been in London, possibly."

Paul looked bewildered. "Then where were we?" he asked.

"Oh, Paul!" exclaimed Carey impatiently. She turned her back on him and watched Miss Price, who had begun once more to dig holes with the trowel. "What are you planting, Miss Price?"

"Edelweiss," said Miss Price absently. She sighed. "Well, all's well that ends well. You were lucky. It might have been worse, a good deal worse."

Carey watched Miss Price insert a silvery plant in the hole, and Charles rolled over sleepily to observe a formation of Valiants against the peaceful sky.

"I thought edelweiss only grew above the snow line," Carey remarked wonderingly.

Miss Price became rather pink and pursed up her lips. "It grows quite well in my garden," she said shortly.

Carey was silent. After she had thought awhile, she said carelessly, "Are you showing anything in the flower show, Miss Price?"

Miss Price's color deepened. "I might show a rose."

"A new rose?" asked Carey interestedly.

"No, a big one," said Miss Price.

"Can we see it?" asked Carey.

"Well, it's still in bud," said Miss Price unwillingly.

"Could we see the bud?"

"Oh dear, Carey," cried Miss Price, suddenly exasperated, "I'm sure it's your lunchtime."

"Not till one o'clock," said Carey reassuringly. "Miss Price."

"Well?"

"If anyone was going for a flower show, would it be fair for them to use magic?"

Miss Price flattened out the earth round the plant with a trowel. She banged it rather hard. "Perfectly fair," she said.

Carey was silent. Paul lay on his face, watching an earwig in the grass. He held one eye open with his finger. He was very sleepy. Miss Price dug another hole.

"What about the people who can't do magic?" asked Carey after a while.

"What about the people who can buy special fertilizers?" retorted Miss Price, jamming the plant in the hole upside down, and then pulling it out again. "What about the people with hothouses?" She shook the plant savagely to get the earth off the leaves. "What about the people who can afford expensive gardeners?" She sat back on her heels and glared at Carey. "How am I to compete with Lady Warbuckle, for instance?"

Carey blinked her eyes. "I only wondered," she said timidly.

"I worked for my knowledge," said Miss Price grimly, starting on another hole. Her face was very red.

"Miss Price," began Carey again after a while.

"Well?"

"Why don't you make a whole lot of golden sovereigns?"

"Of golden sovereigns?"

"Yes, sacks and sacks of them. Then you could buy hothouses and fertilizers and things."

Miss Price sighed. She pushed her hat back a little from her forehead. "I have tried to explain to you, Carey, how difficult witchcraft is, but you still think I just have to wave a wand for anything to happen. Have you ever heard of a rich witch?"

"No," admitted Carey, "I can't say I have."

"Well, I'll tell you why. Money is the hardest thing of all to make. That's why most witches live in hovels. Not because they like it. I was fortunate enough," she added primly, "to have a little annuity left me by my dear mother."

"Aren't there any spells for making money?"

"Dozens. But you can't get the ingredients. What people don't realize," went on Miss Price, "is that there are very few spells that can be done without paraphernalia. You must, if you understand, have something to turn into something and something to turn it *with*."

"Yes," said Carey, "I see." And it was indeed as clear as daylight to her.

"And there are very few spells I know by heart," admitted Miss Price. "I have to have time to look them up. And quiet. I can't be fussed." She took up her trowel again. "If I'm fussed, everything goes straight out of my head. Now you must wake up those boys. There's the church clock striking three-quarters."

Carey got up unwillingly. "I wish," she said, "you'd come with us on the next adventure."

"Well," said Miss Price, "it depends on where you go. If I came, I'd like it a good deal better arranged than last night was, for instance."

"We'd let you choose," offered Carey.

"Well," said Miss Price brightly. "We could all plan it together, couldn't we?" She seemed flustered and pleased at the same time. "But not tonight. Beauty sleep tonight..."

The South Sea island idea came to Carey in the hayloft. She had awakened first and lay sleepily staring at the patch of blue sky through the open door, breathing the sweet smell of the dried apples left over from last year.

"What a pity," she thought, as she stared at the sky, "that we have to go everywhere at night. There are heaps of places I'd like to see, but in daylight." Then slowly she remembered that daylight was not the same all over the world, that the earth was slowly turning, that if you could travel fast enough—in a magic bed, for instance—you might catch up with the sun. The idea gradually took shape and became such an unbearably exciting possibility that she had to wake Charles.

They discussed it at long length, all that evening between tea and bedtime, and the very next morning they tackled Miss Price. Apart from liking her, Carey thought she might perhaps feel safer if Miss Price came along too; a little extra magic couldn't come amiss, and the police station episode had had its frightening moments.

Miss Price was a little alarmed at first at the distance.

"Oh, I can't go gadding about the Pacific at my age, Carey. I like what I'm used to. You'd better go by yourselves."

"Oh, do come, Miss Price," Carey begged her. "You needn't gad about. You can just sit in the sun and rest your ankle. It would do you good."

"Oh, it would be wonderful, Miss Price. Just think—bananas, breadfruit, pineapples, mangoes! You could come on the broomstick."

"The broomstick can only do about five miles at a stretch," objected Miss Price, but her eyes lit up at the thought of a breadfruit cutting in a pot.

"Then you can come with us on the bed. There's heaps of room. Do, do, Miss Price!"

Miss Price wavered. "It would be a change," she admitted.

"Couldn't we go tonight?"

"Tonight!" Miss Price looked startled.

"Well, why not? We slept last night."

Miss Price succumbed. "Well," she said hesitatingly, "if you slept last night . . ."

Paul was a little mystified by the South Sea—island idea, but when Carey and Charles had explained to him the wonders of a coral reef, he, too, became agreeable but insisted on being allowed to take his bucket and spade.

Miss Price got out an atlas and an encyclopedia, and they searched for islands whose dawn would correspond with sunset in England, where European night became Pacific day. They did sums and calculations on the backs of envelopes, and at last they decided on an island called Ueepe. It was not marked on the map, but it was mentioned in the encyclopedia as an island yet to be explored. It had been sighted among others mentioned from the sailing ship *Lucia Cavorta* in 1809 and was spoken of by this name by natives on the island of Panu, four hundred and fifty miles distant, and was said to be uninhabited.

"We'll have the whole place to ourselves," exclaimed Carey delightedly. "We could even rename it."

As it would hardly be possible for Miss Price to sneak into Aunt Beatrice's house so late in the evening and make her way up to Paul's bedroom, it was decided that Miss Price was to come to the window on her broomstick when it began to grow dark and that the children would let her in.

Charles mended Paul's spade for him, and they also found a butterfly net, "which might do for shrimping or anything."

The children undressed and had their baths just as usual, because it was one of those nights when Elizabeth wanted to talk about her sister's little boy's operation. She followed them about from bathroom to bedroom, telling them the well-known details. They knew that later, when she served Aunt Beatrice's dinner, she would sigh and say that she was "worn out getting those children to bed."

But she went at last, stumping down the stairs, and Carey and Charles slipped from their room into Paul's. Paul was asleep, so they sat on his bed and talked in whispers until it began to grow dark. Then they went to the window and watched for Miss Price. Charles was the first to spy her, flying low in the shadows of the cedars. The broomstick had a slightly overloaded look and swayed against the windowsill as a dinghy bumps against a ship's side. It was difficult getting Miss Price in at the window. She was carrying a string bag, a book, and an umbrella, and she dared not let go of the broomstick until her legs were safely over the sill. She knocked her hat off on the lower part of the sash, and Carey, picking it up, found that it was a sun helmet. "My father's," explained Miss Price, in a loud whisper, panting after her exertions, "the one he had in Poona in '99. It has mosquito netting round the brim."

Carey peered at it dimly in the fading light, as it swung upon her finger. It smelled strongly of naphtha. "I don't think there are any mosquitoes in the South Seas," she whispered back.

"Well," replied Miss Price briskly, tying the string bag to the foot of the bed with Paul's dressing-gown cord. "Prevention is better than cure. Better slip the umbrella under the mattress, Charles. And my book, too, please."

It was so dark now that they could hardly see each other's faces. There was no moon, and the cedar boughs were but dim shadows against a gray sky.

Carey wondered suddenly whether they ought to have dressed again. She hadn't thought of it, somehow. Now, it seemed too late. The dark room was full of bustle. Paul was waking as Charles heaved at the mattress to stow away the book and umbrella.

"What do you want?" he asked sleepily.

Carey flew to his side. "Put your dressing gown on," she whispered. "It's time to go."

"To go where?" asked Paul in his normal voice.

"Shush," whispered Carey. "To the South Sea island. The coral reef, you remember?"

"But it's so dark," objected Paul.

"It will be daylight there." She was putting his arms in the sleeves of his dressing gown. "There's a good boy," she praised him. "You've got to say, 'I wish to go to Ueepe.' Here's your net and bucket and spade. I'll take them for you. Kneel up, Paul."

Paul knelt up, facing the head of the bed. Miss Price was firmly tucking in the blankets. She laid her broomstick under the eiderdown. Then they all took their places. Miss Price sat next to Paul, and Charles and Carey held on at the foot.

Paul put his hand on the knob. Then he turned round. "It makes me feel sick, when the bed goes," he announced.

"Oh, Paul," whispered Carey. "It's only a minute. You can bear it. Miss Price has a nice picnic in her bag," she added as an inducement. "Go on. Twist."

Paul twisted. The bed gave a sickening lurch. The night seemed to turn blue, a blue that glittered like a flying tinsel ribbon, a rushing, shimmering blue turning to gold, to light, to heat—to blinding sunshine. Sand flew stinging past their faces as the bed skidded, then bumped, then stopped. They had arrived.

8

The Island of Ueepe

Carey's first thought was that she wished she had brought her hat. The white sand flung back the dazzling glare of the sunlight in such a way that she had to screw up her eyes to see.

The bed had done its best for them. It had set them down on the very tip of a horseshoe-shaped reef. They found themselves on a thin strip of fine white sand held in place by walls of pitted coral. It was almost like being on a ship. In the distance, across a lagoon of dazzling blue sea, they could see the other tip of the horseshoe. In between, a mile or so away, where the front of the horseshoe might be, were trees and low hills.

In among the rocks, which formed the coral walls of their narrow strip of land, were clear pools in which glimmered seaweed of lovely colors, sea anemones, and transparent fish. And the sand was as smooth and fine and white as icing sugar. They had never seen sand like it. There were four great scrapes in it where the bed had come to rest, but beyond that not a footmark, not a ripple.

Charles kicked off his bedroom slippers and let his bare feet sink into the warm crust. It spurted up between his toes. "Gosh," he said happily.

Carey peered over at the lagoon. It was deep and clear. They could see strange fish swimming through the sunlit water. "How lovely!" exclaimed Carey. "How wonderful! Do let's go and explore." Out at sea, between the two points of the horseshoe, great waves rolled up and broke into swirls of spray, spreading their foam into the smooth surface of the lagoon.

Miss Price was unpacking. She took four bottles of ginger pop out of the string bag and placed them in a pool to keep cool. The rest of the food, the hard-boiled eggs and the sandwiches, she put under the bed in the shade.

"You two big ones can explore," she announced, "but I'm going to sit here in the sun." She retrieved her umbrella, her book, and the broomstick. Then sitting down on the sand, with her back against the bed, she methodically removed her shoes and stockings. Miss Price's feet, Carey noticed, were as pink and knobbly as her hands.

"Can we bathe?" asked Charles.

Miss Price adjusted her sun helmet and put up the umbrella. "If you've brought your bathing suits," she said amiably, opening her book.

"We haven't. We didn't think of it."

"Then why ask?" said Miss Price.

Charles and Carey looked at each other. Both had the same thought but neither spoke.

"You can paddle," went on Miss Price, relenting a little. "And explore. I'll take care of Paul."

Paul, on the bed, was leaning over Miss Price's shoulder examining her book. " 'Chapter Six,' " he read aloud slowly. " 'Another Man's Wife.' " Miss Price shut the book on her finger.

"And you, Paul," she said rather sharply, "can take your bucket and spade and build sand castles."

"I'd like to explore," said Paul.

"No, you stay here and play by me. Jump down, and I'll roll up your pajama legs."

In the end it was agreed that Carey and Charles should go off by themselves, each with a bottle of ginger pop, a hard-boiled egg, and a sandwich, and that they should all meet by the bed at about an hour before sunset. "And don't be late," Miss Price warned them. "There's no twilight on these islands."

Carey and Charles raced down the strip of sand toward the mainland. On one side of them lay the still lagoon, on the other the breakers broke on the coral rocks; and as they ran, the children breathed the heady smell of spray. A faint breeze ran up their pajama legs and down their sleeves, an airy coolness on their skin.

"Isn't this gorgeous?" cried Carey, increasing her speed.

"I'll say!" Charles shouted back.

The main beach, when they reached it, was fascinating. They found queer things among the flotsam and jetsam—bits of old spars, a bottle, sharks' eggs. The trees came down almost to the water's edge. A huge turtle scuttled by them into the sea, almost before they realized what it was. There were land crabs among the stones. Under the trees, as they went inland, the ground was smooth, a mixture of earth and sand. They found fallen coconuts and broke them on stones. They nearly went wild with delight when they found their first breadfruit tree. They had read so much about breadfruit.

"I don't think it's a bit like bread," said Charles as he tasted it. "It's more like spongy custard."

They found a freshwater stream, and following it up, through the rocks and creepers, they came to a silent pool. It was a lovely pool, where the roots of trees writhed down into the clear water, and in the middle of it was a smooth and sunlit rock. "For diving," said Charles. They were hot and tired, so, in spite of Miss Price, they threw off their pajamas and bathed.

Once in the water, it was almost impossible to leave it. They dived and swam and sunbathed. They ate their sandwiches and drank their ginger pop. It tasted odd after so much coconut milk. Carey's braids had come undone, and her wet hair streaked about her like a mermaid's. They dozed a bit on the rock and talked, and then they swam again.

"This can be our place for always," said Carey. "Our secret island. I never want to go anywhere else."

There was no hurry to explore it all. They could come back again and again. They could build a house here, bring books, bring cooking things. . . .

When at last they dressed, the sun was lower in the sky and the shadows had crept across the pool. Only in one corner gleamed a patch of golden light. They felt tired as they made their way once more toward the beach, climbing from rock to rock along the bed of the stream. Strange birds flew in and out among the dimness of the trees, and once they heard a hollow, almost human, call. Carey shivered a little in her thin pajamas. Her skin tingled from the sun and water, and her legs felt scratched.

When they came out of the shadows of the trees,

the beach was no longer white but warm gold in the deep glow of the setting sun.

"I think we're a bit late," said Carey. They shaded their eyes with their hands and looked across the lagoon toward the place where they had left the bed. "There it is," said Carey, almost with relief. "But I don't see—" She hesitated. "Can you see Miss Price and Paul?"

Charles strained his eyes. "No. Not unless they're tucked up in bed," he added.

"Then they did go exploring after all," said Carey. "We're back first anyway, even if we are late. Come on."

"Wait a minute," said Charles. He was staring across the lagoon. His face looked odd and blank.

"I say, Carey—"

"What?"

"The water's come up over that bar of sand."

"What?" said Carey again. She followed the direction of his eyes. Smooth rollers were pouring over what had been their path, the spit of sand and coral along which they had raced so gaily that morning; smooth, combed-looking rollers that poured into the smoothness of the lagoon, breaking a little where the coral ridge had held the sand. The bed, black against the glittering sea, stood as they had left it on a rising slope—an island, cut off.

Carey's face, in that golden light, looked expressionless and strange. They were silent, staring out across the water.

"Could you swim the lagoon?" asked Charles after a moment.

Carey swallowed. "I don't know," she said huskily.

"We might try it," Charles suggested rather uncertainly.

"What about Paul and Miss Price?" Carey reminded him.

"They may be tucked up in bed." Charles screwed up his eyes. "It's impossible to see from here."

"You'd see a lump or something. The outline of the bed looks too thin. Oh, dear, Charles," Carey burst out unhappily, "it'll be dark soon."

"Carey!" cried Charles suddenly.

She wheeled round, frightened by the note in his voice. He was looking up the beach toward the shadow of the trees. Three figures stood there, silent, and none of them was Miss Price or Paul; three figures, so still that at first Carey thought they could not be human. Then she shrieked, "Cannibals!" and ran toward the sea. She did not stop to see if Charles was following her; she ran without thinking, without hearing, and almost without seeing, as a rabbit runs from the hunter or the cook from a mouse.

They caught her at the water's edge. She felt their breath on the back of her neck, and then they gripped her by the arms. She screamed and kicked and bit and wriggled. There was nothing ladylike about Carey for quite five minutes. Then, all at once, she gave in. Sobbing and panting, she let them carry her up the beach, head downward. In spite of her terror, she tried to look around for Charles. They had got him too, in the same position. "Charles! Charles!" she cried. He did not, or could not, reply.

The man who had caught her looked exactly like any cannibal she had ever imagined—the lips, the hair, and the nose with a bone stuck through it. He was making for the woods, and at each stride he took, her head bumped dizzily against his spine. He smelled of coconut oil and wore a belt of threaded teeth, which, after a while, she took hold of to steady herself a little as she hung down his back. He held her legs, gripped at the knee in front of his chest. She could see the legs of Charles's captor and glimpses of the third man, who ran along beside them. It was very dark in the woods, and, after a while, she heard the faint sound of drums. Of one thing we may be certain: Carey thought very little of the man who had described the island as being uninhabited. "People should be careful," she almost sobbed, pressing her face against the oily back to keep it out of the way of scratchy creepers, "what they write in encyclopedias."

"Charles!" she called once when it had grown too dark to see.

"I'm here," he shouted back in a panting, suffocated voice.

After a while, as the throb of the drums grew closer, she heard another sound, the chant of human voices: "Ay oh . . . ay oh . . . ay . . . oh . . ." Then she saw a gleam of light. It shone on the boles of trees and the fronds of creepers. It became stronger and brighter until, at last, they found themselves in an open, firelit space where shadows moved and danced, and the earth vibrated to their dancing. "Ay . . . oh . . . ay . . . oh . . . ay . . . oh," went the voices.

It seemed to Carey, from what she could see in her upside-down position, that they had broken through the ring of dancers, because the firelight shone straight in her eyes, and the voices, without changing their tune, swelled to a shout of pleased surprise—"Ay . . . oh . . . ay . . . oh."

Bump. Her captor let her drop on her head, as if she were a sack of potatoes. Dizzily she rolled into a sitting position and looked around for Charles. He crawled up to her. His forehead was bleeding, and he looked quite stunned.

Shining bodies dancing in the firelight, flashing teeth, gleaming eyes. She thought at first they all had hats on, but then she saw it was the way their hair grew. It was ugly dancing, flat-footed with toes upturned, instead of pointed, but even Carey had to admit that it was beautifully in time. Suddenly something pulled her hair. She jumped as if a snake had bitten her. She turned—and there was Paul. He looked very dirty—she could see that even by firelight—but he was smiling and saying something that she couldn't hear because of the noise of drums and voices.

"Paul!" she cried, and suddenly she felt less frightened. "Where's Miss Price?"

Paul pointed—it was the easiest way. There sat poor Miss Price in the very middle of the circle. She was trussed up like a chicken, tied hand and foot with creepers. She still wore her sun helmet and a pair of dark glasses, which glinted in the firelight.

Paul was shouting something in Carey's ear. She leaned closer.

"They're going to eat us," Paul was saying. "They've got the pot back there. They're cannibals."

Carey marveled at Paul's cheerfulness. "Perhaps he imagines it's a dream," she thought wonderingly.

The dance began to quicken. The writhing bodies twisted and swayed. The voices became babbling so that the "Ay . . . oh . . . ay . . . oh" became one word, and the drums increased their speed to a single humming note. There was a sudden shout. Then the dance stopped. There was a shuffling of feet; then silence.

Paul crept up between Charles and Carey. Carey took his hand.

The savages stood quite still, like statues. They all looked inward toward the children. Carey never knew what made her do it, but after a moment's hesitation, she let go Paul's hand and began to clap. Charles followed suit, and Paul joined in, enthusiastically, as if he were at the theater.

The savages smiled, showing their white teeth. They looked quite shy. Then there was a mumble of unintelligible conversation, and everybody sat down cross-legged, like boy scouts round a campfire. Miss Price was in the middle of the circle and nearest to the fire. The three children were grouped together, a little to one side.

After a moment there was a rattle of drums. The circle of eyes turned expectantly toward a path that wound between the trees. Then there was a weird inhuman shout, and a curious figure whirled into the firelight. If it had a face, you couldn't see it for paint. Daubs of scarlet and white hid the features. A great tail of shimmering feathers was attached to his belt at the back, and, as he whirled about, his tail shook as if he wagged it. He wore anklets of monkey's fur, and in one hand he carried a shin-bone and in the other—of all things—Miss Price's broomstick!

"It's the witch doctor," said Charles in Carey's ear. Carey shivered. As she looked round at the seated savages, it seemed as if they had all drawn into themselves, as if they, too, were afraid. The weird object, his legs apart and knees bent, came jumping toward Miss Price. Every jump or so, he would whirl completely round. Each time he wagged his tail Paul laughed.

"Be quiet, Paul," Carey urged him. "You'll make him angry." Paul put his hand over his mouth, but he laughed just the same.

At last the witch doctor stopped, just in front of Miss Price. He threw back his head and made a weird howl, a howl that seemed to echo across the island. Miss Price looked back at him through her dark glasses. The children could not see her expression.

Suddenly, after a moment, there was another howl, higher, weirder, more piercing. The witch doctor lowered the broomstick. There was something about his attitude that seemed bewildered.

Suddenly Carey laughed. She gripped her hands together. "Charles," she whispered excitedly, "Miss Price did it. She did that last one."

The witch doctor recovered from his surprise. He gave two jumps in the air, and then he howled again. It was a howl to end all howls. It went on and on. Carey imagined it echoing out across the reef, across the lagoon, across the darkening sea. Then the witch doctor stopped. He stared at Miss Price. He seemed to be saying, "Beat that if you can."

Miss Price moistened her lips. She wriggled her shoulders as if her bonds constrained her. Then she pursed up her mouth.

This time it was a whistle—a whistle so agonizingly piercing that it hurt one to hear it. It was like a steam engine in anguish, a needlepoint of aching shrillness. The audience began to move, Carey gasped, and the witch doctor clapped his hands to his ears and hopped round as if he was in pain.

When it stopped, there was a murmur among the savages. The witch doctor swung round. He glared at them angrily.

"Hrrmph!" he grunted, and approached Miss Price once more.

She looked back at him impassively. The dark glasses were a great help. Carey crossed her thumbs. She remembered all Miss Price had said in the garden, about how few spells she knew by heart, how everything went out of her head if she were fussed, how you had to have something to turn into something and something to turn it *with*. "Oh, Miss Price!" she breathed, "Miss Price!" as people call the name of their side at a football match.

The witch doctor held up the broomstick; with a twist he flung it into the air. It circled up into the darkness and came down turning slowly. He caught it with his other hand without looking at it.

There was a murmur of approbation among the crowd. They thought that was clever. The witch doctor did a few satisfied jumps.

Miss Price laughed. ("Good," thought Carey. "She isn't fussed.")

The witch doctor glared at her. She sat quite still; curiously still, thought Carey—but something was happening. The children stared hard. There was a space between Miss Price and the ground—a space that grew. Miss Price, still in a sitting position, had risen three feet in the air.

There was a murmur of amazement. Miss Price held her position. Carey could see her teeth were clenched and her face had become red. "Go it, Miss Price," she murmured. "Hold it." She gripped Charles's arm. Miss Price came down, *plonk*, rather suddenly. From her pained expression Carey guessed she had bitten her tongue, but the shock had broken the creepers that bound her hands. Miss Price put her fingers in her mouth as if to feel if her tongue was still there; then she rubbed her wrists and glanced sideways at the children.

The witch doctor did a few wild turns round the circle. He leaped into the air. He shouted, he twirled the broomstick. Carey noticed that every time he came too near the audience, they shrank back a little. When he felt the onlookers were sufficiently subdued and suitably impressed, he stopped his caperings and flung Miss Price's broomstick away from him. He then sat down on his heels and stared at the broomstick. Nothing seemed to happen. The man was still. And so was the broomstick. But there was a waiting feeling in the air, something that prevented Carey from turning her eyes away toward Miss Price.

"*Look*," said Charles suddenly. There was a gasp among the spectators, an amazed murmur. The broomstick was moving, in little jerks as if pulled by a string, toward the witch doctor.

"Goodness!" said Charles. A funny feeling was creeping down his spine. This stirred him more than anything Miss Price had done. Miss Price, too, leaned forward. She pushed her dark glasses up on her forehead. Carey could see her expression. It was the face of one who was deeply and absorbedly interested. Steadily the broomstick moved on toward the witch doctor, who sat as still as a statue made of stone. Silently he seemed to be calling it. If there had been pins on the island, you could have heard one drop.

Miss Price stared a little longer at the broomstick, and then she pulled her glasses down over her eyes again and bent her head. She looked almost as though she had fallen into a doze. The broomstick stopped within a few feet of the witch doctor. It moved no further.

After a moment, the witch doctor raised his head. He looked round the circle, and then he looked back again at Miss Price. She still sat with head sunk forward on her chest. The witch doctor edged himself forward, on his behind, a little closer to the broomstick. "Cheating," whispered Carey furiously.

The broomstick again began to move, but this time it moved away from the witch doctor; not in little jerks, but steadily, surely, it slid toward Miss Price. The man hurriedly resumed his old position. The broomstick stopped.

"Oh, dear," exclaimed Carey. "I can't bear it!"

Then reluctantly, in jerks, it began to move once more toward the witch doctor. Miss Price bent her head still lower and clenched her hands. Carey could see her knuckles shining in the firelight. The broomstick hesitated; then, with a rush, it slid across the sandy ground straight into Miss Price's lap. She gripped it firmly. She threw up her head. The witch doctor leaped to his feet. He gave three jumps, one awful howl, and moved toward Miss Price; in his hand gleamed something long and sharp. Gripping the broomstick, Miss Price faced him sternly. Her feet were tied; she could not move.

Carey cried out and hid her eyes, but Paul, sitting up on his heels, shouted excitedly: "A frog! A yellow frog! Miss Price! You did that lying down!"

Miss Price glanced at Paul, a sideways thankful look. She gasped. Then she held out her two arms toward the witch doctor as if to ward him off with the broomstick. He stopped, with knees bent, about to jump. Then he seemed to shrink and dwindle. He sank downward into his legs as if the heat of the fire was melting him. The children held their breaths as they watched. Every part of him was shrinking at the same time. It reminded Carey of what happened to a lead soldier when you threw it on the fire, but instead of a blob of silver, the witch doctor melted into a minute blob of gold, a tiny yellowish object, barely distinguishable upon the sandy ground.

"You see!" screamed Paul. "She did it! She couldn't do it quickly, but she did it!"

Carey leaned forward, trying to see better. Suddenly the blob jumped. Carey shrieked. Paul laughed. He was very excited. "It's only a frog," he crowed, "a tuppenny-ha'penny little frog...a silly old frog." Carey slapped him.

"Be quiet," she hissed. "We're not safe yet."

There was a strange silence among the savages. They seemed afraid—afraid of the frog, afraid of Miss Price, afraid even of the children.

"Carey!" called Miss Price. She was untying the creepers that bound her feet. Carey ran to her. Charles and Paul followed.

"You'll all have to hold on to the broomstick. It will be hard, but it won't be for long. We must get to the bed. When I shriek, you must all shriek, and that will help the broomstick to rise."

"Four people on a broomstick," gasped Carey.

"I know. It's dangerous, but it's our only hope. Paul can come on my knee, but you and Charles must just hang on. Now don't forget: when I shriek, you all shriek."

Miss Price took Paul on her knee. She gripped the tip of the broomstick with both hands. Carey and Paul took hold of the wood. Miss Price shut her eyes a moment as if she were trying to recall the spell.

The frog had disappeared, but the natives, watching them suspiciously, suddenly began to move forward. Hurriedly Miss Price gabbled her verse:

> "Frog's spawn; toad's eye.
> Newts swim, bats *fly*..."

As she said "fly," her voice rose to a resounding shriek. The children joined in. The broomstick rose a little off the ground. Carey and Charles were hanging by their hands.

"Bats *fly——y——y*," shrieked Miss Price again as a hint to the broomstick. It made a valiant effort. It wobbled slowly upward. The natives ran forward. Knives flashed, but Carey and Charles were just out of reach, dangling. Then Carey saw a man was fitting an arrow to a bow.

"*Fly——y——y,*" shrieked Miss Price again.

"For goodness' sake!" added Charles. His pajama trousers were slipping off. He felt very vulnerable.

Whether or not this unexpected addition to the spell acted as a spur, it is hard to say, but the broomstick gave a sudden leap forward and upward.

The circle of firelight and the gesticulating savages dropped away below them, and they were above the moonlit trees, and there ahead lay the glimmer of the sea. The broomstick swayed and plunged but kept its course, making for the point of the reef. Carey and Charles hung on for dear life. Their arms felt numb and almost pulled from their sockets, and a cold wind whistled through their nightclothes.

Above the lagoon, the broomstick swerved; sickeningly it began to circle downward. Carey and Charles floated up sideways as the broomstick dived. Carey strained her eyes. She could only see breakers, breakers and spray and moonlit waters. Was the bed submerged? "Oh," she cried, as the broomstick gathered speed, making straight for the waves. Then suddenly she saw the bed. It was not yet under water. It stood just where they had left it on the rising strip of sand. But as they landed, she saw a great wave swell up, gather height, and curl.

"Wish, Paul, wish," shrieked Carey madly. Then the wave broke over them. Gasping, spluttering, soaked to the skin, they clung to the slippery bed rails.

Paul must have wished. The bed rolled and lurched, then spun into space. The darkness thinned as they whistled through it. A pale light grew around them, deepening to gold, and rose and blue and yellow—flowers, twisted into nosegays and tied with blue ribbon. . . . Carey stared, and then she recognized the pattern. It was the early sunlight shining on Paul's wallpaper. . . .

9

Account Rendered

They were home, but what a mess! All their pajamas were ragged and dirty, their dressing gowns lost, and the bed was soaked. Poor Miss Price was a sorry sight. Her sun helmet was soft and soggy. She had no shoes or stockings, and her coat and skirt dripped puddles on the floor. Of her belongings, all she had left was the broomstick. Haggardly, she peered out of the window.

"It's too light to fly," she muttered. Then an awful thought seemed to strike her. "It must be after nine o'clock." She sat down limply on a chair. As she sat, she squelched. "Goodness me, Carey, here's a nice to-do!"

Charles went to the window. It was open, just as they had left it.

"There's no one about," he said. "Just use the broomstick as far as the ground and then make a run for it."

Miss Price stared at him blankly. "Oh, dear," she exclaimed, "this is terrible."

"Yes, Miss Price, you must," urged Carey, "make a run for it."

Miss Price looked at her naked bony feet. "If I should meet the gardener..." she pointed out helplessly.

"You must risk it," said Carey.

"Listen!" whispered Charles, raising his head.

Yes. Unmistakably there were footsteps coming upstairs.

"Quick, Miss Price." Carey pushed the broomstick into Miss Price's unwilling hand. They helped her over the sill.

"Oh, dear," Miss Price muttered to herself as gingerly she clung to the coping. "This is not the way to do things."

"I know," whispered Carey, giving Miss Price a little shove, "but it can't be helped."

They watched Miss Price float slowly down; then they watched her pick up her skirts and the broomstick and make for the shelter of the bushes. They drew a sharp breath of relief as she reached cover, and then they turned—to face the eyes of Elizabeth.

"Breakfast," said Elizabeth, standing in the doorway, "has been on the table this half hour—"

She paused. Then her mouth fell open. She was staring at the floor. Carey, looking downward, saw a large black puddle spreading slowly from the bed toward Elizabeth's feet. Elizabeth's eyes followed the stream to its source. Her mouth opened wider, and her gaze traveled slowly from the bed to the children. It took in their appearance from top to toe, the smudged faces, the wet hair, the peeling noses, the torn pajamas clinging limply to the sun-scorched limbs.

"Well—" said Elizabeth slowly, "I never!" Then she shut her mouth with a snap. Her eyes glared. Color mounted slowly to her pallid cheeks. "This," said Elizabeth, "is the end."

Deliberately she looked round once more. She picked up a corner of the eiderdown. It was dark red instead of pale pink. It hung heavily between her thumb and forefinger. Regular clocklike drips drummed gently on the polished floor. She let it fall. She stared at it a moment unbelievingly, and then once more she looked at Paul and Carey. She smiled, a grim, menacing little smile that did not reach her eyes. "All right," she said calmly and, turning, left the room.

The three children stood quiet. In silence and misery they stood while the puddles deepened round their feet and the drips from the eiderdown

ticked off the heavy seconds. At last Carey moved.
She pushed back her wet hair.

"Come, Paul," she said huskily. "Let's go to the
bathroom and wash."

"What I don't understand," said Aunt Beatrice for the fourth time, "is from where you got the water. The bathroom's right down the passage, and there isn't a jug."

The children gazed back at her. They were in the study. Aunt Beatrice sat at her desk turning a little sideways so that she could face them as they stood in a row on the carpet. There was a closed look in their faces, though their eyes were round and candid. "*Whatever happens,*" Carey had warned them, "we mustn't give away Miss Price. Except for that, it doesn't matter what we say because nothing could be worse."

Carey cleared her throat. She did not reply but stood staring unwaveringly at her aunt's face.

"The charitable attitude to adopt, Carey," said Aunt Beatrice in her precise, cutting voice, "is that you are not quite right in your head. This story about a South Sea island, cannibals... lagoons... If it were necessary to lie, a child of three could do better."

Carey swallowed.

"A magic bed..." Aunt Beatrice smiled acidly. "It might interest you to know, Carey, that I bought that bed myself in 1903, quite new, from Baring & Willow's—a most reputable firm," she added, "and not given to innovations."

Carey changed her weight from her left foot to her right.

"What I still don't understand," reiterated Aunt Beatrice, "is from where you got the water."

"From the sea," said Paul suddenly. "Carey told you."

Aunt Beatrice raised her almost hairless eyebrows. She picked up her pen and turned back to her desk. Her thin smile was far from reassuring.

"No matter," she said. "I have wired your mother, and Elizabeth is packing your things—the last service Elizabeth will perform for me. After all these years she has given me notice."

"But it's true, Aunt Beatrice," Carey burst out. "It was the sea. You can prove it."

Aunt Beatrice half turned, the pen delicately suspended in her birdlike hand.

"How, may I ask?" she inquired ironically.

"By licking the blanket, Aunt Beatrice," said Carey politely.

Aunt Beatrice's pink-rimmed eyes became like agates.

"You are not my children," she said coldly, "and I am not as young as I was; there is no reason at all why I should put up with this sort of thing! Your mother, job or no job, must make other arrangements for you. I have finished. You may go."

They crept to the door. At the threshold they paused; Aunt Beatrice was speaking again. "As there are no taxis," she was saying, "Mr. Bisselthwaite, the milkman, has very kindly consented to pick you up at eleven forty-five at the end of the lane. Your train leaves at twelve."

Gently, gently they closed the door.

10

Farewell

The milkman was late. "Perhaps," said Carey, as they stood in the grass by the side of the lane, "we could just run in and say good-bye to Miss Price."

"One of us had better stay," said Charles, "to look after the bags and wait for the milk cart. You and Paul go."

Carey hesitated. "All right," she said, after a moment. "And you can come along in the cart."

Miss Price was in her front garden. When she saw Carey and Paul in coats and hats, she looked surprised. She set down her wheelbarrow and waited between the shafts. Carey ran up to her.

"Miss Price," she said, "we're going."

"Going where?" asked Miss Price. Her face looked tired and rather pale except for the sunburn on her long thin nose.

"Home. To London."

"Oh, dear," said Miss Price. She looked distressed. She began to pull off her gardening gloves.

"It was the bed and the water and everything. We're being sent away. But we did keep our promise, Miss Price. We never told about you."

"Oh, dear," said Miss Price again. She sat down on the edge of the wheelbarrow.

Paul, very subdued, began to collect dead flower heads from the rubbish.

"We came to say good-bye," went on Carey.

"Oh, dear," said Miss Price for the third time. "I feel very much to blame. We shouldn't have gone to that island, but," she went on, "I thought a nice quiet day, a breath of sea air . . ." She paused.

"Look," Paul broke in. "A pink cabbage."

Carey looked down. There it lay among the rubbish, Miss Price's giant rosebud!

"Oh, Miss Price—" exclaimed Carey, staring at it. It must have weighed a couple of pounds.

Miss Price colored. "I have done a lot of thinking since yesterday, Carey. I've been thinking about last night and what you said about the flower show—" She glanced at Paul as if to include him in her observations. "I've been thinking that magic may be a kind of cheating. It looks good to start with, but perhaps it doesn't bring good results in the end."

Paul frowned. "I've had wonderful results from cheating," he said stubbornly.

"I don't suppose I'll give it up altogether," went on Miss Price, ignoring Paul and holding on to her gentle smile. "But I thought I'd try to give it up for a while."

They were all silent. "Oh, Miss Price," murmured Carey rather sadly. She shared Paul's disappointment.

"It gets such a hold on one," said Miss Price.

There was an awful pause. Paul had turned back the leaves of the pink cabbage. A sweet dry smell of sun-warmed deadness rose from the barrow.

"I have decided," went on Miss Price, watching Paul's fingers, "in future to regard witchcraft—not as a hobby"—she paused—"but as a weakness."

"Darling Miss Price," cried Carey suddenly, "you're such a good sport." She flung her arms round Miss Price's neck. She felt the wetness of a tear on Miss Price's long nose. "Thank you, Miss Price, for everything, even the cannibals."

It was a moving moment. Paul looked glum, a little bewildered. He had an uneasy feeling that Miss Price was turning over a new leaf before he had finished with the old one. It was almost a relief when the milk cart rattled up to the gate. Miss Price wiped her eyes.

"Now you must go," she said, straightening her hat as Charles jumped down off the milk cart to shake her hand. She tried to smile. "Good luck, dear children, and good-bye. Keep your warm hearts, your gentleness, and your courage. These will do," said Miss Price, sniffing audibly, "just as well as magic."

She turned away hurriedly; squaring her shoulders, she picked up the handles of the wheelbarrow and trundled it off toward the rubbish heap.

The milkman cracked his whip, and they clattered away amid the cheerful jangle of empty cans.

"She won't keep it up," said Paul, who, unobserved, had edged himself into the place nearest the pony.

In the train, Charles frowned through the narrow square of window. Carey had told him of the conversation with Miss Price.

"Magic may be just a weakness," he said, "but it's better than some weaknesses."

"I know," agreed Carey.

"If we still had the bed, I think I'd use it," Charles went on. "Sometimes."

"Yes," said Carey. "Just sometimes."

"The bed wasn't magic," put in Paul consolingly. "It was only the bed-knob that was magic."

"Well, it's the same thing," said Carey, turning irritably from Paul, who, kneeling up on his seat, was breathing in her face. "One thing's no good without the other."

"Couldn't you use a magic bed-knob on another bed the same make?"

"Oh, I don't know, Paul." Carey edged away from him, closer to the window. "What's the good of talking about it if we haven't got either? Do sit down properly!"

Paul meekly put his legs down, so that they dangled just above the floor. He leaned back, sucking his cheeks in. One hand was in his pocket, fidgeting. He looked worried. "But," he protested, after some moments of silent thought, "I did bring the bed-knob."

II

BONFIRES AND BROOMSTICKS

1

Lost and Found

Two years went by. Aunt Beatrice died and the
house was sold, so they did not go back to Much
Frensham. The memory of that summer became a
secret thing, seldom spoken of—and never with
Paul. "He might tell, you see," Carey pointed out.
"We must let him just think it's a dream..."

Sometimes in company Paul could become a
menace. "When we were in prison—" he would exclaim, and Carey, blushing, would correct him
quickly with, "When you *dreamed* you were in
prison, Paul!" After a while, Paul grew confused; he
would say—one eye on Carey—things like: "Yesterday, when I dreamed I had an egg for tea—"

"But you did have an egg for tea," his mother
would point out.

"Oh," he would say, becoming suddenly thoughtful, "and did I see the cannonballs?"

"What cannonballs?"

"Cannibals, he means," Carey would explain quickly. "No, you didn't, Paul. You dreamed those," and would quickly change the subject.

Even to Charles, the thing became unreal. Back among his school friends, just the word became embarrassing. Magic? One didn't...one couldn't... I mean, the whole thing was rather...He took up boxing, started on First Year Latin, and began a stamp collection. He pushed other events to the back of his mind and pretended they had not happened.

One cannot do this successfully. It seldom works; sooner or later Fate takes a hand, and back comes the past like a bombshell. It came to Carey and Charles, some two years later, on a cold, dull winter's morning, in the form of a daily paper. It came in innocently with the bacon and porridge, disguised as the *London Times*.

"Look," said Carey faintly. She was leaning over, spoon in hand, reading the personal column.

Charles glanced up. They were alone in the room at the time. Mrs. Wilson, their mother, had left for her office, and Paul was not yet down. There was a strange expression on Carey's face; she seemed more than a little scared. "What's the matter?" asked Charles.

Carey pushed the paper across. "See," she said, pointing with her finger.

He did not see at first. "Mink coat," he read aloud, "scarcely worn . . ."

"No, below that."

"Pale hands, my heart is singing . . ."

"No, here." She leaned over him, her braids snaking on the table. "Lady with small house . . ."

"Lady with small house in country willing accommodate two schoolchildren summer holidays. Moderate terms. Highest references. Reply E. Price, Much Frensham . . ." Charles's voice grew slower. ". . . Beds."

There was silence.

"Now do you see?" asked Carey.

Charles nodded. They were silent again.

"Little Alders?" said Charles after a moment. "Was that the name of the house?"

"Something like that. I can't quite remember."

"There must be lots of Prices in Much Frensham," protested Charles.

"But E. Price," said Carey. "Miss Price's name was Eglantine."

"Was it?" said Charles. He, too, had become a shade paler.

"Yes. Eglantine Price," repeated Carey firmly.

They stared at each other without speaking. Then once more they leaned over the paper.

"It says only two children," Charles pointed out.

"Oh, Paul can sleep anywhere, if she knows it's us, don't you think?"

Both minds were working furiously. With a mother who was tied to her office, there was always this problem of the long summer holiday. Last year, they had gone to a farm in Cornwall and had enjoyed it very much; there seemed no reason why they should not be sent there again.

"But Much Frensham's much nearer London," Carey pointed out. "Mother could get down to see us. And when we tell her that Miss Price was a friend of Aunt Beatrice's—"

"Not a friend exactly."

"Yes. Remember the peaches?"

Charles was silent. "What about the bed-knob?" he said at last.

"What about it?"

"Where is it?"

Carey's face fell. "I don't know." She thought a moment. "It must be somewhere."

"Why? Heaps of things in this house aren't anywhere. I'd as soon go to Cornwall," Charles went on, "as go to Miss Price's without the bed-knob."

"Well, I would too," admitted Carey—at least

there were beaches in Cornwall . . . and caves, and rock climbing. She thought a moment. "Once it was in the knife box."

"It isn't now."

"Or was it the tool drawer?"

"Yes, it was in the tool drawer for ages. After they redid the nursery cupboards, remember? It isn't now."

"I don't know," mused Carey. "I've seen it somewhere—in a box or something. There were some old door handles, and some screws . . ."

"Old door handles?" exclaimed Charles. "I know where those are."

"Where?"

Charles jumped to his feet. "That canvas bag on a nail in the broom cupboard . . ."

That was just where it was—a little rusty and spotted with whitewash. They took it as a "sign."

Mrs. Wilson was puzzled. Bedfordshire instead of Cornwall? And why this undercurrent of excitement about so very *un*-exciting a maiden lady? There was more in this, she suspected uneasily, than appeared on the surface. But to all her questions, they gave the most satisfactory replies. Miss Price, as a holiday chaperone, sounded almost too good to be true. Letters were exchanged and a meeting was arranged.

The children mooned about in a torment of suspense. They need not have worried, however. Over tea and cakes with Miss Price at Fuller's, their mother's fears were laid. Although unable to discover the secret of Miss Price's peculiar charm, Mrs. Wilson found her just as Carey had described her—

quiet, reserved, a little fussy. Dignified but friendly, she expressed a guarded fondness for the children and her willingness to accommodate all three, provided they would be careful of her belongings and would help a little in the house.

"How wonderful . . . how wonderful!" sang Carey when she heard the news. She went on singing and dancing about the room, and even Charles felt impelled to try a handstand. Only Paul remained stolid. He sat on the hearth rug, watching them curiously.

"Will we sleep there?" he asked his mother, at last.

Mrs. Wilson turned to look at him—too bland, his face seemed, almost too candid. "Yes, Paul," she said, in a puzzled voice, "of course you will sleep there . . ." Again, for some reason, she began to feel uneasy. "Why?"

Paul began to smile. It was a slow smile, which spread gradually over all his face. He turned away and began plucking at the carpet. "Oh, nothing," he said lightly.

2

And Lost Again

When they arrived at the station, it looked at first as though there was no one to meet them. Then Carey saw the milk cart on the far side of the level crossing. "Come on," she said, "there's Mr.—Bisselthwaite." She was surprised when the name came so easily to her tongue. Mr. Bisselthwaite the milkman . . . of course.

"She ordered an extra two pints," Mr. Bisselthwaite told them, as they climbed on the cart. "And she said it was you. Growed, hasn't he?" he added, nodding at Paul.

"We all have," said Carey. The train had gone, and the station was quiet. The grass by the roadside smelled of clover, and high up in the sky a lark sang. "Oh, it's lovely to be back in the country!"

Clop-clop-clop went the pony. The scent of horse mingled with the scent of fields, and deep country stillness spread away on all sides.

"There's Tinker's Hill," said Charles. Tinker's Hill? How oddly these names came back. And the Roman Remains. "Look, Paul, that grass-covered sort of wall—that was a Roman fortress once."

Paul gazed at the hazy green of the rounded hillside. It seemed to him far away and, at the same time, quite close. It was part of the lovely dream of riding in a milk cart instead of in a taxi, part of the *clip-clop* of the pony's hooves on the flinty road, part of the rhythmic rise and fall of the dusty piebald back and the light swift rattle of the wheels.

"Miss Price's house is there, Paul," said Carey, "under that hill. You can't see it yet. Oh, you see that lane? That goes to—to Body-something Farm."

"Lowbody Farm," said Mr. Bisselthwaite.

"Lowbody Farm. Oh, and there's Farr Wood—"

"Look, Paul," broke in Charles. "You see those cedars—those dark trees just beyond the church spire? Well, Aunt Beatrice's house is in there. Where we stayed last time."

"The Water Board took it over," said Mr. Bisselthwaite.

"Oh," said Carey. "When?"

"About a twelvemonth after your aunt died."

"Oh," said Carey again. She was silent for a while, trying to imagine the dark old house without Aunt Beatrice; without the high sideboards and the

heavy curtains; without the rugs and the tables and
the palms in pots; without the ...

"Mr. Bisselthwaite!" she said suddenly.

"Well?"

"Did the Water Board take the furniture?"

"No, the furniture was sold."

"Who to?"

"Well, there was a sale like. Dealers from London came down. And the village bought a bit. My
old woman bought a roll of linoleum and a couple of
chairs."

"Oh," said Carey.

So the furniture had been sold. Someone, somewhere, all unknowing, had bought Paul's bed, was sleeping on it at night, making it in the morning, stripping back the sheets, turning the mattress . . .

"Was everything sold?" Carey asked. "Beds and all?"

"I reckon so," said Mr. Bisselthwaite. "The Water Board wouldn't want no beds. Whoa, there," he called, bringing the pony to a walk. "Know where you are now?"

It was the lane—Miss Price's lane that ran along the bottom of Aunt Beatrice's garden. Carey's heart began to beat as she saw a bright cluster of rambler roses among the hawthorns of the hedge, Miss Price's Dorothy Perkins—the ones that twined across her gate. They were thicker, higher, more full of bloom than they had been before. And here was the gate with LITTLE ALDERS painted on it in white. She glanced at Charles. He, too, looked slightly nervous.

"Well," said Mr. Bisselthwaite as the pony came to a standstill, "here we are. I'll give ye a hand with the bags."

The gate squeaked a little as they opened it, and the latch clanged. They walked as if in a dream down the straight paved path between the flower beds, which led to the front door. It was silly, Carey told herself, to feel afraid.

The door opened before they touched the knocker, and there before them was Miss Price. It was almost a shock. Miss Price—fresh and smiling, and rather flushed. "I heard the gate," she explained, taking Carey's bag. "Well, well, well. This *is* nice! Careful of the step, Paul; it's just been cleaned." She was as they remembered her, and yet, as people do when you have not seen them for a long time, she seemed somehow different. But something about her long pink nose comforted Carey suddenly. It was a kind nose, a shy nose, a nose that had had a tear on the tip of it once (so long ago it seemed); it was a reassuring nose; it was Miss Price.

A delicious smell of hot scones filled the little hall. Miss Price was saying things like: "Wait a minute while I get my purse...Paul, how you've grown...Put it down there, Mr. Bisselthwaite, please, just by the clock...Three and six from ten shillings is...Paul, don't touch the barometer, dear. The nail's loose...Now let me see..."

And then Mr. Bisselthwaite was gone, and the front door was closed, and there was tea in the dining room, where the square table took up all the space and the chairs neatly touched the walls. There were scones and jelly and potted meat. And there, through the lace curtain, beyond the window, was Tinker's Hill, steeped rich and gold in the afternoon sunshine, and Carey suddenly felt rested and happy and full of peace.

After tea Miss Price showed them their rooms.

It was a small house, neither old nor new. There were brass stair rods on a Turkey carpet, and at the top of the stairs a picture of "Cherry Ripe." Carey's room was very neat, but there were a lot of things stored there as well as the bedroom furniture. Cardboard boxes were stacked on top of the wardrobe, and a dressmaker's dummy, shaped like an hourglass, stood behind the mahogany towel rack. But there was a little jar of mignonette on the dressing table, and a spray of dog roses in a vase on the mantelshelf. Charles's room was neat too—and barer. It had an iron bed and cream-painted furniture. It had probably been a maid's room.

"Paul, I'm afraid," said Miss Price, "must sleep on the sofa in my bedroom. You see, I only said two children in my advertisement, but"—she smiled round at them quickly and made a little nervous movement with her bony hands—"I never thought—I never dreamed it would be you."

"Weren't you surprised?" asked Carey, coming up to her. They were standing beside Charles's bed.

"Yes, yes, I was surprised. You see, I'm not very fond of strangers. I had to have someone."

"Why?" asked Paul.

"The rising cost of living," explained Miss Price vaguely. Then, in a sudden burst of frankness: "It was putting in the new kitchen sink, really. Stainless steel, you know. And what with the plumbing... well, anyway, that's how it was. And, on the whole, I prefer children to adults. Through the *Times,* I thought I might get two well-brought-up ones..."

"And you got us," said Carey.

"Yes," agreed Miss Price, "I got you. Had we only known," she went on brightly, "we could have done it all without advertising at all. Now you two had better unpack. Where are Paul's things?"

"They're mostly in with Charles's," said Carey. "Miss Price."

"Yes?"

"Could we—could we see the rest of the house?" A watchful look came over Miss Price's face. She folded her hands together and glanced down at them.

"You mean the kitchen and the bathroom?"

"I mean—" said Carey. She took a deep breath. "I mean—your workroom."

"Yes," said Paul eagerly, "could we see the stuffed crocodile?"

Miss Price raised her eyes. There was an odd trembling look around her mouth, but her glance was quite steady.

"There is no stuffed crocodile," she said.

"Alligator, he means," put in Charles.

"Nor alligator," said Miss Price.

There was a moment's embarrassed silence. All

three pairs of eyes were fixed on Miss Price's face, which remained tight and stern.

"Oh," said Carey in a weak voice.

Miss Price cleared her throat. She looked around at them as if making up her mind. "I think," she said in a thin kind of voice, "it would be better if you did see my workroom." She felt in the pocket of her skirt and brought out a bunch of keys. "Come along," she said rather grimly.

Once more, after two long years, they were in the dark passage by the kitchen; once again Miss Price was putting a key in a well-oiled lock, and, as if in memory of that other time, Carey's heart began to beat harder and she clasped her hands together as if to stop them trembling.

Miss Price stood aside on the threshold. "Come in," she said. "Go right in."

The children filed past her and then they stood silent, gazing at the shelves.

"Well?" exclaimed Miss Price sharply. "It's very nice, isn't it?"

"Yes," said Carey huskily.

There was no alligator; no chart of the zodiac; no exercise books; no newts' eyes; no boxes that might have held dried mice. Instead there was row upon row of bottled fruits and vegetables in every shade of color, from the pale jade of gooseberries to the dusky carmine of pickled cabbage.

Miss Price ran her finger along the labels: "Tomatoes, apple pulp, plums, greengages, elderberries—they mix very well with black currants. Do you know that?"

"No," said Carey, "I didn't."

"Red currants, sliced pears, tarragon in vinegar, green tomato chutney...What's this? Oh, I know—mushroom catchup. The label's come off." She held the jar to the light. "Looks a bit mottled—" She pushed the jar back out of sight. "Some of these are last year's," she explained hastily. "Red currants, loganberries, and rose-hip cordial." She rubbed her hands together. "Well?" she said again, as if waiting for praise.

"It's—" Carey swallowed. "It's very nice."

Paul's eyes were round and his face unhappy. "Where's the crocodile?" he asked bluntly.

Miss Price colored. "You see, Paul, I—"

Carey came quickly to her rescue. "People don't keep things for always, Paul." She glanced at the shelves. "Think of the puddings! Think of the lovely, lovely puddings."

"Yes," said Paul.

"You see, Paul," said Miss Price more calmly,

"sometimes people do things for a bit and then they give them up. Smoking, for instance. People often give up smoking."

Paul looked bewildered.

"And drink. People give up drink."

Paul looked still more puzzled. Miss Price smiled at him very kindly. "Haven't you ever given up sugar in your tea for Lent?"

Paul blinked his eyes. "Yes, but—"

"You see, Paul," interrupted Carey sharply, "Miss Price has given up alligators. Come on, now." She began to pull him toward the door.

"Forever?" persisted Paul.

Miss Price nodded her head. "Forever and ever," she said.

"Or just for Lent?" put in Paul.

Miss Price glanced at him swiftly. It was a strange look, almost startled; she seemed struck by a sudden idea.

"Lent is over," she said, but seemed to hesitate. Then once more she became firm. "No," she went on. "Forever and ever. If we do things, it shouldn't be by halves."

"But anything's all right," said Charles, "in moderation."

"Not magic," said Miss Price.

"You once said even magic."

"Did I?" asked Miss Price. "Did I really say that?"

"Yes, you did. I remember quite well."

"Did I really?" said Miss Price pensively. "Well. Anyway," she added quickly, "come along now. It's nearly Paul's bedtime. Careful of the step."

Charles wandered out into the garden while Carey bathed Paul. He leaned over the back fence and stared at Tinker's Hill. So she had given up magic! That was what came of looking forward to something too much—a feeling of flatness and disappointment. Finding the bed-knob, which at the time had almost seemed a "sign," now only added to the sense of loss. He thought of Cornwall, and of mackerel fishing; of rocks and coves and beaches at low tide. Oh, well, he told himself, we're in the country anyway. There would be walks and explorations, and there was always the river. There might even be a boat. And then he felt something move under his shoe. It was a mole, diving upward through the soft earth and hitting the exact spot where he had placed his foot. In a minute he was on his knees, pulling up the coarse sods of grass that grew down there beside the fence. He dug with his hands into the soft earth, throwing it aside as a dog does, and did not notice Carey until she stood beside him.

"What are you doing?"

"Digging for a mole." He sat back on his heels. "I say, Carey—" He looked up at her face and paused. "What's the matter?"

Carey's expression was odd. She looked half afraid. "I want you to come and look at something," she said.

"Let me just finish this!"

"You'll never catch it now." She paused. "This is important."

"What is it?" asked Charles, half getting up.

"Come and see."

"Can't you tell me what it is?"

Carey turned away and began walking toward the house. Charles followed her. As they reached the front door, he said: "You might tell me—"

Carey turned right round, putting her finger to her lips.

"Ssh—" she said.

"Where's Miss Price?" asked Charles in a loud whisper.

"Ssh—" said Carey again. "She's in the kitchen. Making macaroni cheese. Come on."

He followed her up the stairs.

"It's in here," said Carey, "where Paul sleeps." She threw open a door.

It was Miss Price's bedroom. Very clean, very neat, very fragrant. A large photograph of a military gentleman hung over the mantel. There were silver brushes on the dressing table and a porcelain "tree" for rings. Paul was tucked up in a bed on the sofa, a small Victorian couch with a curved back that just fitted him.

"Well, it's all right," said Charles, staring at Paul, who looked unusually clean and round-eyed.

"What's all right?" asked Carey.

"Paul's bed."

"I wasn't looking at Paul's bed," said Carey.

Charles followed the direction of her eyes. Miss Price's bed had a white embroidered spread, and a black silk nightdress case lay on the pillow. It was an exciting nightdress case, closely related to a tea cozy, trimmed with satin blobs like colored fruit.

"You are dense," said Carey. "The bed itself!"

Charles stared.

It was a very ordinary brass bed—a bed like a hundred others. But where at its head there should have been a second bed-knob, the right-hand post ended in a piece of rusty screw.

"Yes," said Charles. He sat down rather suddenly on the foot of Paul's sofa.

"Is it, do you think?" asked Carey anxiously.

Charles cleared his throat. "Yes," he said soberly, "yes, it must be!"

"There are hundreds of beds like that. She may

have had it for years. She may have bought it at the same time as Aunt Beatrice bought hers."

"Yes," said Charles. He seemed dazed. "But the screw. I think it is. It must be it. She must have bought it at the sale." He turned to Carey. "We can easily tell. Go and get the bed-knob."

"That's just it," said Carey. "The bed-knob's gone!"

"Gone?"

"Yes. When I'd finished bathing Paul, Miss Price had done the unpacking. I've been through everything. You can look yourself. It's gone."

"She's taken it," said Charles.

"Yes, she's taken it."

"Oh, gosh!" said Charles. There was a world of disillusion and sadness in his voice.

Paul lay staring at them glumly over his neatly turned-down sheet.

3

In for a Penny

Yes, now they were there "the cupboard was bare!"
Oh, it wasn't that she wasn't glad to see them; it
wasn't that she wasn't very kind and had made up
that lovely bed for Paul on the sofa in her room. It
wasn't that she didn't plan delightful picnics to Pepperinge Eye and Lowbody Farm, and the Roman Remains; and read to them at night, and teach them
croquet. It was just that she had given up magic.
She seemed to have given up for good and all. She
seemed to have forgotten that she ever knew it.
Right behind the bottled fruits in the larder Paul did
once see some pink and blue, which he thought
might be the chart of the zodiac, but he didn't get a
chance to look properly as the door was nearly always kept locked.

All their excitement, all their planning, seemed
to have gone for nothing until one day—

It was Carey's job to put the cleaned shoes by

each person's bed at night all ready for morning. About a week after they had arrived, when she had forgotten them the night before, she had to creep down before breakfast to fetch Paul's shoes from the scullery. As Paul slept on the sofa in Miss Price's room, it meant that Carey had to open that door very, very quietly so she could slip in without waking Miss Price. Well, that was the morning when she found Miss Price's bed had gone.

A faint (the very faintest) film of dust and a pair of quilted slippers marked the place where it had stood. The coverlet was neatly folded on the chest of drawers, and not another thing was out of place. Paul's clothes lay tidily upon his chair, his sofa stood in its usual corner, but Paul himself was nowhere to be seen.

Carey ran down to the passage to call Charles, and he came with her, slowly and sleepily, to see the empty room. They talked it over. They could hardly believe it.

"I told you it was the bed," Charles reminded Carey. "I knew it by that piece of rusty screw."

"But behind our backs!" exclaimed Carey. "To have pretended to have given up magic, and then to go and do a thing like this—behind our backs."

As Carey dressed, she grew angrier and angrier. She cleaned her teeth so viciously that she made the gums bleed. She nearly exploded when she heard the bump in Miss Price's room, and Paul's cheerful voice asking if there were raspberries for breakfast.

But barely had she and Charles sat down at table when Miss Price appeared, followed by Paul. Miss Price, looking brisk and neat, and not at all out of the ordinary, went straight to the sideboard to serve the porridge. Paul, who looked as if he had dressed hurriedly, sidled into his place. Except for his unbrushed hair and pullover back to front, he, too, looked quite normal. When Miss Price came to the table with the porridge, there was a look of exhilaration about her as if she had had a cold bath. "A lovely day," she said cheerfully as she poured out the coffee. She smiled round the table at the children. "What are we going to do with it?"

Carey's face became wooden. "We haven't thought," she said coldly.

"What about a picnic lunch on the Roman Remains?" suggested Miss Price, undaunted.

"I don't think people should picnic on Roman remains," said Carey.

Miss Price gave her a curious look, and then she turned to Charles. "Have you any suggestions, Charles?"

"What is Paul going to do?" asked Charles suspiciously.

Miss Price looked a little taken aback. "Why, go with you. Unless, perhaps, you go to the Roman Remains. That is a little far—"

"I think," said Charles, "we should go somewhere where Paul can come too."

Miss Price looked surprised. "Well, of course, that would be nicer. I just thought—that sometimes you and Carey like to do things on your own—"

"No," said Carey firmly, "we like Paul with us. Always."

Miss Price looked really surprised at this. And so did Paul. He sat with his porridge spoon aslant, dripping milk down the front of his jersey.

"Paul!" said Miss Price sharply. Paul came to and swallowed the porridge, and Miss Price wiped off the drips.

"Well, children," said Miss Price at the end of breakfast, "you must make your own plans. I have my music lessons, but I shall be free by lunchtime. Go to the bathroom, please, Paul."

Carey and Charles went out in the garden to wait for Paul.

He emerged with a burst almost immediately, his voice raised in a tuneless rendering of "Hark the Herald Angels Sing." Quickly and silently Charles and Carey took him each by an arm and pulled him through the hedge into the meadow. They walked him out of earshot of the house, and then they sat him down in the long grass, still holding him.

"Paul," said Carey sternly, in a fair imitation of Aunt Beatrice's voice, "it's no good hedging. Charles and I know all."

Paul looked bewildered and tried to pull his arms free.

"You and Miss Price," went on Carey, "have been off on the bed. It's no good lying. Charles and I saw."

Paul looked unperturbed. "Did you see us go?" he asked.

"Never mind," said Carey darkly.

Paul, sensing their mood, sat still. He just looked bored like a pony tied to a stall.

"Well?" said Carey. "What have you to say?"

It seemed Paul had nothing to say. He fidgeted with his feet and did not look even interested.

"Have you been often?"

"No," said Paul, making a not very determined effort to pull his wrist free, "we were only trying it."

"Is this the first time you've tried it?"

"Yes."

"Did it work all right?" asked Charles. He sounded more friendly suddenly.

"Yes."

Carey let go Paul's wrist. "Where did you go, Paul?"

Paul smiled.

"Tell us, Paul," urged Carey. "We're sure to find out."

"Guess," said Paul.

"All right. You must answer 'yes' or 'no,' and you can say 'sort of.'"

"Was it in the western hemisphere?" asked Charles.

"No," said Paul.

"Was it the eastern hemisphere?" asked Carey.

"No," said Paul.

"Then it wasn't in the world!" exclaimed Charles.

"Yes. It was in the world," said Paul.

"Well, then it must have been in the western or the eastern hemisphere."

"No," said Paul. "It wasn't anywhere like that."

"He doesn't know what hemisphere means," Charles suggested.

Paul looked stubborn. "Yes, I know what it means."

"What does it mean?"

"Well—it means— It doesn't mean Blowditch."

"Is that where you went?"

"Yes."

"You only went as far as Blowditch?"

"Yes."

"Why, you could walk there," exclaimed Charles.

"It was only to see if it worked," explained Paul.

"Did you ask Miss Price if you could try it?"

"No. She asked me. She said, 'Let's give it a little twist. I don't suppose it still works.'"

"Spells don't wear out," said Carey.

"How do you know?" asked Charles.

"Well, it stands to reason," replied Carey.

They were silent awhile. Then Carey said tolerantly, "I can understand how it happened. But I don't think it's at all fair. And I never have thought it fair that Paul was the only one who could work it."

"Well, it was his knob," said Charles. "We mustn't grumble. There are people who would give anything for a magic bed-knob, whoever had to work it."

"Yes," agreed Carey, "I know. But, as they've had a turn, I think we ought to have a turn too. Miss Price can do as she likes for herself, but *we* never said we'd give up magic."

"I don't see how we could manage it," said Charles, "not with the bed in Miss Price's room."

Carey tossed back her braids. "I shall just go to Miss Price in a straightforward way and ask her right out."

Charles, slightly awed, was silent.

"And there's another thing," Carey went on. "Do you remember that when Miss Price gave us the spell, she said that if we turned the knob backward the bed would take us into the past? Well, I think she ought to let us have one go at the past. After that, we could give it up—for a bit," she added, "though I don't see what all this giving up of magic does for anybody. You'd think it might be used for the defense scheme or something."

"Carey!" exclaimed Charles, deeply shocked.

Carey, a little subdued, broke off a stalk of sorrel and chewed it pensively. "I suppose you're right," she admitted after a moment. She had sudden visions of dragons breathing fire and mustard gas and whole armies turning into white mice. It would be terrible, unthinkable, to have one's brother, say, invalided out of the army as a white mouse, kept for the rest of his life in a cage on the drawing room table. And where would you pin the medals on a mouse?

"You see," said Charles, "Miss Price is quite right in some ways. You can overdo things."

"I know," Carey admitted. "But I don't see how it would hurt anybody if we just had a little trip into the past."

"Well, there's no harm in asking," said Charles.

They cornered Miss Price after supper. She listened to their argument; she saw the justice of what they said; but she threw up her hands and said, "Oh dear, oh dear!"

They tried to reassure her; they were very reasonable and very moderate. "Just one more go, Miss Price, and after that we'll give it up. It's a pity to waste the past."

"I don't like it," Miss Price kept saying. "I don't like it. If you were stuck or anything, I couldn't get you out. I've burned the books."

"Oh, no—" cried Carey, aghast.

"Yes, yes, I burned them," cried poor Miss Price. "They were very confidential."

"Can't you remember anything by heart?"

"Nothing to speak of. One or two little things . . . Oh dear, this is all my fault. I just wanted to see—out of simple curiosity—if spells wore out. I never dreamed it would start all this up again—"

"Please let us try, Miss Price," urged Carey. "Just this once, and we'll never ask again. We did keep our word, and you're not really keeping yours if you don't let us just *try* the past. We never told anyone about your being a witch, and now, if you won't let us use the spell again anyway, it wouldn't matter if we did tell—"

"Carey!" exclaimed Miss Price. She stood up.

Her eyes gleamed strangely. Her long thin nose suddenly seemed longer and thinner. Her chin looked sharper. Carey drew away alarmed.

"Oh, Miss Price," she muttered nervously.

"If I thought"—went on Miss Price, leaning her face closer as Carey backed away—"if, for a minute, I thought—"

"You needn't think," cried Carey agitatedly. "We wouldn't ever tell. Ever. Because we promised and we like you. But," she added bravely, "fair's fair."

Miss Price stared at Carey a moment or two longer; then, limply, she sat down again in her chair. Her hands lay open on her lap. Tired, she seemed suddenly, and sad. "Professionally speaking," she said, "I'm no good. I should have put a rattling good spell on all three of you and shut you up once and for all." She sighed. "Now it's too late."

Nervously Carey took Miss Price's limp hand in hers. "You needn't worry about us," she said reassuringly, "you really needn't."

"And you were wonderful," exclaimed Charles warmly, "professionally speaking."

"Do you really think so?" asked Miss Price uncertainly.

"Yes, Miss Price, we do," affirmed Carey. "Don't be discouraged. You'll pick it all up again, easy as pie, once you set your mind to it."

"You think I will?" asked Miss Price wanly. "You're not just saying that?"

"I know it," said Carey, nodding her head.

Miss Price patted her hair as if she felt it had come out of place. "I hope you're right," she said, in her usual voice. "And in the meantime, as you have had some experience, and providing you went somewhere really *educational* and took *every* precaution and were very, *very* careful, I don't see"—she looked at them gravely, almost speculatively, and she drew in her breath—"how *one* little trip into the past could hurt anyone."

4

The "Past"

In London, during the reign of King Charles II, there lived a necromancer. (****** These six stars are to give you time to ask what is a necromancer. Now you know, we will go on.) He lived in a little house in Cripplegate in a largish room at the top of a narrow flight of stairs. He was a very nervous man and disliked the light of day. There were two good reasons for this; I will tell you the first.

When he was a boy, he had been apprenticed to another necromancer, an old man from whom he had inherited the business. The old necromancer, in private life, was fat and jolly, but in the presence of his clients he became solemn as an owl and clothed his fat whiteness in a long dark robe edged with fur so that he could fill them with respect and awe. Without his smile, and in his long dark robe, he looked as important as a mayor and as gloomy as a lawyer's clerk.

The young necromancer, whose name was Emelius Jones, worked very hard to learn his trade. It was he who had to turn out at ten to twelve on cold moonlit nights to collect cats from graveyards and walk the lonely beaches in the gray dawn seeking seven white stones of equal size wet by the last wave of the neap tide. It was he who had to mash up herbs with pestle and mortar and crawl down drains after rats.

The old necromancer would sit by the fire, with his feet on a footstool, drinking hot sack with a dash of cinnamon, and nod his head saying: "Well done, my boy, well done..."

The young necromancer would work for hours by candlelight, studying the chart of the heavens and learning to read the stars. He would twist the globe on the ebony stand until his brain, too, rotated on its own axis. On sweltering afternoons he would be sent out to the country on foot to trudge through the fading heather, seeking blindworms and adders and striped snails. He had to climb belfries after bats, rob churches for tallow, and blow down glass tubes at green slime till the blood sang in his ears and his eyes bulged.

When the old necromancer was dying, he sent for his assistant and said, "My boy, there is something I should tell you."

Emelius folded his stained hands in his lap and dropped his tired eyes respectfully. "Yes, sir," he murmured.

The old necromancer moved his head so that it fitted more comfortably into the pillow.

"It's about magic," he said.

"Yes, sir," replied Emelius soberly.

The old necromancer smiled slyly at the carved ceiling. "There isn't such a thing."

Emelius raised a pair of startled eyes. "You mean—" he began.

"I mean," said the old necromancer calmly, "what I say!"

When Emelius had got over the first sense of shock (he never completely recovered), the old necromancer went on:

"All the same, it's a good-paying business. I've kept a wife and five daughters out at Deptford (whence I shall be carried tomorrow), with a carriage and four, fifteen servants, French music teacher, and a bark on the river. Three daughters have married well. I have two sons-in-law at court and a third in Lombard Street." He sighed. "Your poor father, may he rest in peace, paid me handsomely for your apprenticeship; if I have been hard on you, it is from a sense of duty toward one who is no more. My affairs are in good order, my family well provided for, so the business as it stands and these premises I leave to you." He folded his hands on his chest and became silent.

"But," stammered Emelius, "I know nothing. The love philters—"

"Colored water," said the old necromancer in a tired voice.

"And foretelling the future?"

"Child's play," murmured the old necromancer, "if you don't go into details; whatever you prophesy about the future comes true sooner or later, and what doesn't come true, they forget. Look solemn, don't clean out the room more than once a year, brush up your Latin, oil the globe so that it spins smoothly—and may good luck attend you."

That is the first reason why Emelius was a nervous type of man. The second was because in the reign of good King Charles it was still the fashion to send witches, sorcerers, and all those who were reputed to work magic, to the gallows, and Emelius, if he made a slip or an enemy, might at any moment be delivered by an unsatisfied client to a very tight and uncomfortable end.

He would have got out of the business if he dared, but all the money of his patrimony had been dispensed in learning magic, and he was not a strong enough character to start afresh.

In the year 1666 Emelius, at thirty-five, had become old before his time, old and thin and terribly nervous. He would jump if a mouse squeaked, turn pale at a moonbeam, tremble at his servant's knock.

If he heard a footstep on the stairs, he would immediately begin a little spell, something he knew by heart, so that his clients might be impressed as they entered by his practice of magic. He had also to be ready to sit down at the clavichord, in case it was a king's man come to spy upon him, and pretend he was a dreamy musician who had inherited the necromancer's lodging.

One evening, hearing footsteps in the narrow hall below the stairs, he leaped up from the chair where he had been dozing by the fire (these late August nights held the first chill of autumn), trod on the cat (which let out an unearthly squeal), and seized a couple of dried frogs and a bunch of henbane. He lit a wick, which floated in a bowl of oil, sprinkled it with yellow powder so it burned with a blue flame, and hurriedly, with trembling hands, rushed off a little spell—with one eye on the clavichord and the other on the door, and all his body poised for instant flight.

There was a knock, a hesitatingly fumbled knock.

"Who's there?" he called, preparing to blow out the blue flame.

There was a whisper and some shuffling; then a voice, clear and treble as a silver bell, said, "Three children who are lost."

Emelius was taken aback. He made a movement toward the clavichord, then he came back to the blue flame. Finally, he stood between the two, with one hand carelessly poised upon the globe, in the other a sheet of music. "Enter," he said somberly.

The door opened, and there, thrown into relief against the dark passageway, stood three children, strangely dressed and dazzlingly fair. They wore long robes after the style of the London apprentice, but tied by silken cords, and their cleanliness, in seventeenth-century London, seemed not of this world. Their skins shone, and Emelius's quivering nostrils detected a delicate fragrance, as of fresh flowers strangely spiced.

Emelius began to tremble. His knees felt unsteady. He wanted to sit down. Instead he looked unbelievingly toward the paraphernalia of his spell. Could two dried frogs and a bunch of henbane do this? He tried to recall the gabble of Latin he had said over them.

"We are lost," said the female child in that strange foreign voice, clear-cut as rock crystal. "We saw your light burning, the street door was open, so we came up to ask the way."

"Where to?" asked Emelius in a trembling voice.

"Anywhere," said the female child. "We are quite lost. We don't know where we are."

Emelius cleared his throat. "You are in Cripple-gate," he managed to say.

"Cripplegate?" said the female child wonder-ingly. "In London?"

"Yes, in London," whispered Emelius, edging away toward the fireplace. He was terribly afraid. From whence had they come if they did not know they were in London?

The elder male child took a step forward. "Excuse me," he said, very civilly, "could you possibly tell us what century we are in?"

Emelius threw up trembling hands before his face as if to ward off the sight of them. "Go back, go back," he implored, in a voice broken by emotion, "from whence you came."

The female child turned pink and blinked her eyelids. She looked round the dim and cluttered room, with its yellowing parchments, its glass vials, the skull on the table, and the candlelit clavichord.

"I'm sorry," she said, "if we are disturbing you."

Emelius ran to the table. He picked up a bowl with oil, the two frogs, the twisted henbane, and with an oath he threw them on the fire. They spluttered, then flared up. Emelius rubbed his fingers together as he watched the blaze, as if to rid them of some impurity. Then he turned, and again his eyes widened so that the whites showed. He stared at the children.

"Still here?" he exclaimed hoarsely.

The female child blinked her eyes faster. "We will go at once," she said, "if you would just tell us first what year it is——"

"The twenty-seventh day of August, in the year of Our Lord 1666."

"1666——" repeated the elder male child. "King Charles the Second——"

"The Fire of London will take place in a week's time," said the girl child brightly, as if she were pleased.

The elder boy's face lit up too.

"Cripplegate?" he said excitedly. "This house may be burned. It will start at the king's baker's in Pudding Lane, and go on down Fish Street——"

Emelius suddenly fell on his knees. He clasped his hands together. His face was anguished. "I implore you," he cried, "go, go . . . go . . ."

The girl child looked at him. Suddenly she smiled, with kindness, as if she understood his fear. "We won't harm you," she said, coming toward him. "We're only children—feel my hand."

She laid her hand on Emelius's clasped ones.

It was warm and soft and human. "We're only children—" she repeated. "Out of the future," she added. She smiled at her companions as if she had said something clever.

"Yes," said the elder boy, looking pleased and rather proud. "That's what we are, just children out of the future."

"Is that all?" said Emelius weakly. He got to his feet. He spoke rather bitterly. He felt very shaken.

Now the youngest child stepped forward. He had a face like an angel with dark gold hair above a white brow. "Could I see your stuffed alligator?" he asked politely.

Emelius unhooked the stuffed alligator from the ceiling and laid it on the table without a word. Then he sat down in the chair by the fire. He was shivering a little as if with cold. "What else is about to come upon us," he asked gloomily, "besides the fire that will burn this house?"

The little girl sat down on a footstool opposite him. "We're not awfully good at history," she said in her strange way. "But I think your king gets executed."

"That was Charles I," the elder boy pointed out.

"Oh, yes," said the little girl. "I'm sorry. We could go back and look it all up."

"Do not give yourselves this trouble," said Emelius glumly.

There was a short silence. The little girl broke it.

"Have you had the plague?" she asked conversationally.

Emelius shuddered. "No—thanks be to a merciful Providence."

"Good show," exclaimed the elder boy heartily.

The little girl, asking permission, poked the fire to a brighter blaze. Emelius threw on another log. He stared miserably at the broken bowl blackened by burning oil. The old necromancer had doubly deceived him, for he, Emelius, quite by accident, had found a spell that worked. These children seemed comparatively harmless, but another mixture, lightly thrown together in the same irresponsible way, might produce anything—from a herd of hobgoblins to Old Nick himself.

And it wasn't as if he knew the antidotes. Whatever came would come to stay. He would never feel safe again. Never more would he dare throw sulfur on the fire with muttered imprecations; never more would he dare boil soups of frogs' spawn and digitalis; never more reel off Latin curses or spin the globe of the heavens into a dizzy whirl of prophecy. His uncertainty would manifest itself before his clients. His practice would fall off. His victims might turn against him. Then he would have to fly, to hide in some filthy hovel or rat-infested cellar, or it might mean prison, the pillory, the horsepond, or the rope.

Emelius groaned and dropped his head into his hands.

"Don't you feel well?" asked the little girl kindly.

Emelius kicked the log further into the blaze. Then he raised haggard eyes to the little girl's gentle face.

"A child..." he said wonderingly. "I never knew"—he dropped his voice sadly—"what it was to be a child."

"Oh, you must have known!" exclaimed the elder boy reasonably.

"Did you always live in the town?" asked the little girl.

"No," said Emelius, "I lived in the country. I should have said," he went on, adventuring into truth, "that I had *forgotten* what it was to be a child."

"Well, you're pretty old," remarked the elder boy consolingly.

Emelius looked stung. "Thirty-five summers!" he exclaimed.

"Have you had a sad life?" asked the little girl.

Emelius raised his eyes. A sad life. Ah, he thought to himself, that's what it is—I have had a sad life. Suddenly he longed to tell of his life. The years of fruitless labor, the dangers of his profession, its loneliness. He could talk with safety to these strange children who (if he managed to hit on the right spell) would disappear again into the future. He pulled his fur-trimmed robe up over his knees away from the fire, showing coarse yellow stockings, which hung upon his legs in wrinkles.

"There are few lives," he began rather gloomily, but as if he might be going to warm up later, "sadder than mine . . ."

Then, in quaint words and phrases, he told the children of his childhood, the childhood he said he had forgotten; of how he had been sent out, at an early age, to gather herbs and simples; of the old schoolmaster who had taught him; of May and Maying; of a man who had stood in the stocks for poaching; of being beaten for stealing sugared plums; of how he had hated the nine times table and had worn a dunce's cap for Latin. Then he went on to his apprenticeship in London, the hardships and the disillusionment; the fear of starting on his own; the terror in which he lived; and the people who wouldn't pay their bills.

As the children listened, the candles grew long shrouds of wax and the fire died low. So absorbed were they in the story that they did not hear the watchman cry the hours or note the presence of dawn behind the curtain.

"Yes," concluded Emelius with a sigh, "my father's ambition was his son's undoing. In truth I have amassed some small store of gold, but would I had remained a simple horse doctor in the vale of Pepperinge Eye."

"Of Pepperinge Eye," exclaimed the little girl. "That's close to where we're staying."

"In Bedfordshire," said Emelius, his gaze still caught up in the past.

"Yes. Near Much Frensham."

"Much Frensham," said Emelius. "Market day at Much Frensham . . . then were great doings!"

"There are still," said the little girl excitedly. "I dare say there are lots of new houses, but the main road doesn't go through there, so it isn't much changed."

They began to exchange impressions. Emelius it seemed had bathed in their brook; Lowbody Farm had still been called Lowbody Farm; "a fine new residence," Emelius called it, and he, too, had roamed the short grass on the tiered mound known as Roman Remains.

"Five of the clock," called the watchman, as he passed below the window, "and a fine, clear, windy morning."

They drew back the curtains. The dim room shrank from the clear light, and dust danced golden in the sunbeams.

"I wish you could go back to Pepperinge Eye," cried the little girl. "I wish you could see it as it is now."

Then they, in their turn, told him of their lives, of the war, of their first visit to the country, of the magic bed. They told him how they had left the bed a few yards down the road in a walled churchyard. It was then they remembered the string bag, tied fast to the bed rail, with the cheese sandwiches and the thermos of hot cocoa. Emelius, his housekeeper being still "abed," was much put to it to find food, but at length he produced from the larder two legs of cold roast hare and a jug of beer. He was deeply relieved to hear that it was no spell of his that had called these children from the mysteries of the future and was more than anxious to go with them to the churchyard so that he might see the bed.

They set out, a strange procession, Emelius carrying the jug of beer with the hare wrapped neatly in a napkin. The yard gate was open, and there, behind the biggest tomb, they found the bed just as they had left it, with the string bag tied securely to the foot.

It was there they had their early breakfast, while the hungry cats prowled around and the city slowly woke to the clang and rumble of a seventeenth-century day. And it was there, without mentioning her name, that they told about Miss Price.

5

A Visitor

Miss Price slept in Carey's room the night the children were away. She had a restless night. She was not feeling at all happy about having let them go off on their own. She had been caught between two sets of fairnesses. What was fair, she thought, to the children was hardly fair to their parents. Besides, a trip into the past could not be planned with any degree of accuracy. They had seen first how many twists the bed-knob allowed, and then they had made a rough calculation of period. They had aimed for the time of Queen Elizabeth, but goodness knew what they had got. Charles rather cleverly had made a scratch with a pin, from the side of the knob, across the crack, and down the base of the screw. And when Paul twisted, he was supposed to twist until the two ends of the scratch met evenly. All very rough and ready, as neither Miss Price nor the children knew if the period covered by the bed-knob embraced the beginning of the world or just the history of England from 1066 onward. They had assumed the latter.

"Oh, dear," muttered Miss Price to herself, tossing and turning in Carey's bed. "If they come back safe from the trip, it will be the last, the very last, I shall allow."

She had tried to be careful and to take all sensible precautions. The bedclothes had been carefully folded and put away and the mattress covered by a waterproof groundsheet. She had provided the children with a thermos of hot cocoa, bread and cheese, and a couple of hard-boiled eggs. She had given them an atlas and a pocket first-aid kit. Should she have furnished them with a weapon? But what? She had no weapon in the house barring the poker and her father's sword.

"Oh, dear," she muttered again, pulling the bedclothes round her head as if to shut out a persistent picture of the children timidly wandering through a bleak and savage England inhabited by *Diplodocus Carnegii* and saber-toothed tigers. And that Neanderthal man, she told herself unhappily, would be utterly useless in an emergency. . . .

Toward morning she fell into a heavy sleep and was awakened by the sudden opening of the bedroom door. The bright sunshine streamed in through the partially drawn curtains, and there, at the foot of her bed, stood Carey.

"What time is it?" asked Miss Price, sitting bolt upright.

"It's nearly nine o'clock. The boys are dressed. I didn't like to wake you—"

"Thank heaven you're back safely!" exclaimed Miss Price. "You can tell me all your adventures later. Is breakfast ready?"

"Yes, and the boys have started. But—" Carey hesitated.

Miss Price, who had put her feet out of bed and was fumbling for her slippers, looked up.

"But what?"

"We've got to lay another place," said Carey uncomfortably.

"Another place?"

"Yes—I, we— You see, we brought someone home with us."

"You brought someone home?" said Miss Price slowly.

"Yes—we thought you wouldn't mind. Just for the day. He needn't stay the night or anything." Carey's eyes seemed to plead with Miss Price. She grew pinker and pinker.

"He?" repeated Miss Price.

"Yes. His name is Emelius Jones. Mr. Jones.

He's a necromancer. He's awfully nice, really, underneath."

"Mr. Jones," echoed Miss Price. She hadn't had a man staying in the house since her father died, and that was more years ago than she cared to remember. She had forgotten all their ways, what things they liked to eat and what subjects they liked to talk about.

"What did you say he was?" asked Miss Price.

"He's just a necromancer. We thought you wouldn't mind. He lived near here once, with an aunt. We thought you'd have a lot in common."

"Who's going to take him back?" asked Miss Price. She frowned. "No, Carey, I do think this is thoughtless of you. I had made up my mind this was the last trip the bed was going to make, and there you go picking up strange necromancers who you know perfectly well have to be taken home again, which means another journey." She pushed her feet into her bedroom slippers. "Where did you say he was?"

"He's in your bedroom," said Carey. "On the bed."

Miss Price looked really put out. "Oh, dear," she said. "Whatever next?" She slipped her arms into her blue flannel dressing gown. "How am I to get my clothes, or do my hair, or anything? I really am annoyed, Carey!" She gave a vicious tug as she tied up her dressing gown. "You must take him down to breakfast, and I'll have to see about him later."

Emelius meekly followed Carey down the stairs. He looked dazed and gazed wanly about him. As he took his place at the breakfast table, he staggered slightly against Paul, who was halfway through his porridge.

Carey looked worried. "Mr. Jones, are you all right?"

"Yes, I am well enough."

"You look so pale."

Emelius ran a limp hand across his windblown hair. "Small wonder," he remarked, smiling faintly.

Carey gazed at him uneasily; she was thinking of Miss Price. Would he, she began to wonder, give quite the right impression? In the bright light of day Emelius looked far from clean: his tousled hair hung wispily about his ears and his pallid skin was grayish. The long thin hands were stained, she noticed, and the nails were rimmed with black. The velvet of his fur-trimmed robe, though rich, was sadly spattered; and when he moved, he smelled of cottage kitchens.

There was no time to do anything about it, however; Miss Price came in almost immediately, looking slightly flustered. She was wearing her best pink blouse, the one she kept for trips to London. Emelius rose to his feet—long and thin, he towered above the table.

Miss Price, in one swift glance, took in his appearance from top to toe. "So this is Mr. Jones?" she remarked brightly—not, it seemed, to anyone in particular.

"Emelius Jones. Your servant, madam. Nay"—he bowed deeply—"your slave—"

"How do you do," put in Miss Price quickly.

"—humbly content," Emelius persisted, "to raise his eyes to one whose subtle craft, maturing slowly through the ages as a plant in the dark earth spreads its roots and sucks its sustenance, bringing forth shoot and stem and branching foliage to burst at length into dazzling blossom, blinding in this your twentieth century the reverent gaze of one who dared to doubt..."

Miss Price, blushing slightly, moved to her place behind the teapot. "Oh, well," she exclaimed, and gave a little laugh, "I wouldn't say that exactly. Do you take milk and sugar?"

"You are bountiful," exclaimed Emelius, gazing at her spellbound.

"Not at all. Do sit down."

Emelius sat down slowly, still gazing. Miss Price, her lips pursed, poured out two cups of tea in thoughtful silence. As she passed his cup, she said conversationally, "I hear you have an aunt in these parts?"

"And a house," put in Carey quickly. To establish Emelius as a man of property might help, in Miss Price's eyes, to enhance his status. "At least, it will be his. On Tinker's Hill . . ."

"Really?" remarked Miss Price. She sounded dubious. She helped herself to a boiled egg and began to tap it thoughtfully. "Is there a house on Tinker's Hill?"

"Yes, indeed," Emelius assured her, "a comely, neat house—with an apple orchard."

Miss Price looked noncommittal. "Really?" she said again, then, remembering her manners, "Porridge, cornflakes, or rice crispies?"

He took porridge. Again there was silence— only comparative: Emelius was a noisy eater and not, Carey noticed, a very tidy one. When he drank down his tea in a series of gulps (as though it were medicine, thought Carey), Miss Price tightened her lips and glanced at Paul. "You had better get down, dear," she said.

"I haven't finished," complained Paul.

"Eat up, then. Quickly."

Paul, nothing loath, gobbled noisily, copying

Emelius. Miss Price, averting her face, took a dainty spoonful of boiled egg, which, closing her eyes, she consumed very slowly. "Oh dear," thought Carey, who knew this sign. She glanced sideways at Emelius, who, having peeled one egg and eaten it whole, was reaching for another. He picked off the shell abstractedly, deep in thought. Suddenly he gave a large belch.

Miss Price opened her eyes, but she did not change her expression. "Some more tea, Mr. Jones?" she asked sweetly.

Emelius looked up. "Nay, I am well enough," and, as he thought they seemed puzzled, he added quickly, "but 'tis an excellent infusion. None better. And good they say against the Falling Sickness."

"Really?" said Miss Price again, and hesitated. "Some toast and marmalade?"

"Marmalade?"

"It's a preserve made from oranges."

"Ah, yes, indeed," exclaimed Emelius, "I am very partial to it." He took the cut-glass dish, and, using the jam spoon, quite unhurriedly he scraped it clean. Paul was fascinated; his eyes seemed to bulge and his mouth fell open.

"Now, get down, Paul," Miss Price said quickly when he seemed about to speak; and she turned again politely to Emelius who, more relaxed, was leaning back in his chair thoughtfully licking the jam spoon. "The children tell me you are interested in magic?"

He laid down the spoon at once, all courteous attention. "Yes, that is so. It is, as one might say, my calling."

"You practice for money?"

Emelius smiled, shrugging slightly. "For what else?"

Miss Price, quite suddenly, looked pleasantly flustered. "I don't know . . . You see—" Her face became quite pink. "A real professional! I've never actually met one . . ."

"No?"

"No." Miss Price hesitated, her hands clasped together in her lap. "You see—I mean—" She took a long breath. "This is quite an occasion."

Emelius stared. "But you, madam—do you not practice for money?"

"I? Oh dear me, no." She began to pour a second cup of tea. "I'm only an amateur—the merest beginner."

"The merest beginner . . ." repeated Emelius, amazed. He stared even harder. "Then—if I understand rightly—it was not you, madam, who caused the bed to fly?"

"The bed-knob? Yes, that was me. But"—she

laughed a little deprecatingly, sipping her tea—"it was quite easy really—I just went by the book."

"You just went by the book," repeated Emelius in a stunned voice. He drew out an ivory toothpick and, in a worried way, began to pick his teeth.

"Yes." (Carey felt happier now: Miss Price was almost prattling.) "I have to measure everything. I can't do a thing out of my head. I'd very much like to *invent* a spell. That would be so worthwhile, don't you think? But somehow . . ." She shrugged. "You, I dare say," she went on, dropping her voice respectfully, "have invented many?"

For one panic-stricken moment, Emelius caught Carey's eye. He quickly looked away again. "No, no—" he declaimed. Then, seeing Miss Price's expression, he added modestly, "None to speak of." He gazed in a hunted way about the room and saw the cottage piano. "That's a strange instrument," he remarked, as though to change the subject.

Miss Price got up and went toward it. "Not really," she explained, "it's a Bluethner." As Emelius came beside her, she raised the lid of the keyboard. "Do you play?"

"A little."

He sat down on the music stool and struck a few notes, half closing his eyes as though listening to the tone. Then, head nodding and fingers skipping, he swept into a little piece by William Byrd. He played with great feeling and masterly restraint, using the piano as though it were a harpsichord. Miss Price seemed quite impressed.

"That was very nice," she admitted guardedly. And, glancing quickly at her watch, she moved away and began to clear the table.

"It was lovely," cried Carey warmly, as she jumped up to help. "Do play some more!"

Emelius, turning to look at her, smiled a trifle wanly. "*Saepe labat equus defessus,*" he explained, glancing at Miss Price.

Miss Price looked back at him, her face expressionless. "Yes, quite," she agreed uncertainly.

"Or perhaps," Emelius went on, "one might more truly say '*mira nimia oculos inebriant*'?"

"Well," said Miss Price and gave a little laugh, "it's as you like, really," and she clashed the plates together rather noisily as though to make a distraction.

"I think," said Charles uncertainly, aside to Miss Price, "that perhaps he means he's tired..."

Miss Price blushed warmly, immediately all concern. "Oh, dear, oh dear...of course; how stupid of me! Charles, dear, put a chair under the mulberry tree for Mr. Jones; he can rest there quietly..." She glanced about the room. "And we must find him something to read. Where's the *Daily Telegraph*?"

They could not find the *Telegraph* but found instead a book called *Little Arthur's History of England*. "Couldn't he have this?" Charles urged. "It would be even better. I mean, it would be all news to Mr. Jones from chapter seven onward."

They went out through the back way for Emelius to see the kitchen. Surprised and delighted, he admired all the right things in the right way—the electric cooker, the plastic plate rack, and the stainless steel sink. He clothed his wonder in odd, poetical phrases. Miss Price seemed very pleased. "I can't afford a refrigerator—at least, not yet," she told him as he ran a loving hand across the gleaming surface of the sink. "But this is rather jolly, don't you think? Forty-three pounds, seven shillings and tenpence, excluding the plumbing. But worth it in the end, wouldn't you say?"

But it was in the garden that Emelius came into his own. His knowledge of plants astounded even Miss Price, and he told her countless uses for what had seemed the commonest of herbs. Mr. Bisselthwaite's boy, who was delivering the milk, broke off his whistling to stare at Emelius. Emelius, his long velvet robe sweeping the lawn, returned the milk-boy's stare with somber dignity. The whistling was resumed, and the milkboy clanged down the two pints with his usual roughness.

Later, leaving Emelius with a history book in the shade of the mulberry tree, reading with much interest of what was to come to pass in his future, Charles and Carey sought out Miss Price in her bedroom.

"Miss Price," whispered Carey, as if Emelius might hear, "do you like him?"

Miss Price, who was making up the bed, paused, sheet in hand. "He has distinction," she admitted guardedly.

"Think, Miss Price," went on Carey, "of the things you'd have to talk about. You haven't even begun—"

Miss Price wrinkled her forehead. "Ye-s," she said uncertainly.

"Couldn't he stay a bit longer? Couldn't he stay a week?"

Miss Price turned. She sat down suddenly on the edge of the bed. "I had better be perfectly frank," she announced firmly. "He could only stay on one condition."

"What condition?" they asked excitedly.

The tip of Miss Price's nose became rather pink.

"He must be persuaded to have a good hot bath," she said. "And he must have a haircut."

"Oh, I'm sure he'd do it. Willingly," said Carey.

"And his clothes must go to the cleaners."

"But what will he wear meantime?"

Miss Price looked thoughtful. "There's that old Norfolk suit of my father's, and ... yes, I've some things in a trunk ..."

Carey and Miss Price were not present when Charles tackled Emelius under the mulberry tree, but in the still summer air the sound of their voices floated in through the open window. Charles's voice was a burbling monotone, but Emelius's was raised. Charles's suggestions were meeting with opposition. The conversation went on and on. There were a few deep silences. Carey shut her eyes and crossed her thumbs; the going, she realized, was not easy. At last, through the mist of leaves, she saw Emelius stand up. As the two figures began to approach the house, Carey drew back into the room, but not before she heard Emelius's parting shot, delivered in a voice that broke. "So be it," he said, "if it is the custom, but I had an uncle died of the ague through this same cause."

Preparing Emelius's bath was something of a ceremony. Miss Price dug out her fluffiest and softest bath towel and a clean cotton kimono with an embroidered spray of flowers across the back. Carey ran the water to a pleasant, even temperature and threw in a handful of Miss Price's carefully hoarded bath salts. She spread out the bath mat and closed the window. Emelius was ushered in, the plumbing was explained to him by Charles, and he was asked to put his clothes outside the door.

He was a long time in the bath. The children tiptoed around the house in a state of nervous anxiety, as if a major operation was taking place upstairs. After a while, they heard him running the hot and cold taps and raising his voice, against the sound of the water, in a little Shakespearean ditty, slightly off-key.

"He's enjoying it," said Charles.

Emelius bathed, his soft mouse-colored hair falling carelessly across his brow, looked almost ten years younger. And there was an old-fashioned distinction about the Norfolk suit. It fitted him quite well; Miss Price's father, Carey realized, must have been as thin and angular as Miss Price. The buckled shoes, perhaps, were not quite right, but the overall effect was pleasing; he looked rather romantic, or—as Charles put it—"like some kind of poet from Oxford."

Miss Price examined him with critical eyes and, on the whole, seemed pleased. With comb and nail scissors, she lightly trimmed the hair behind his ears. "That's better," she said, as she brushed him down. Modestly proud, she seemed, as though she had invented him. "Now let me see your nails..."

Emelius submitted humbly to being turned about—to having his tie knotted and his collar straightened; this was his homage to a master craftswoman—one who would always know best.

They arranged to make tea a picnic meal and to take Emelius across the fields to Pepperinge Eye. It was with no small excitement that they started out on this expedition. Miss Price herself looked strangely moved as Emelius with sparkling eyes named each field or wood. There were few changes. Rush Field, Stummets, Cankerho, these had been the same in his day. Blowditch in Emelius's time had been called Bloodyditch, an echo of past battles, but Farr Wood was still Farr Wood, "and still," said Carey, who had walked there often, "as far." Emelius could not find his father's house in Pepperinge Eye. He thought it had stood on the site of the present vicarage. They all insisted upon going into the churchyard to see if, by any chance, Emelius had been buried there. But he wasn't—at least he couldn't find his own grave. He found, however, the grave of his aunt—Sarah Ann Hobday—and to his surprise, after scraping the lichen from the nearly defaced gravestone, he found that she had died on the twenty-seventh of August, 1666, the day—was it yesterday?—on which the children had appeared in his rooms. It was like getting a telegram.

"Oh, dear," said Miss Price, distressed, "I am so sorry. Perhaps we had better go home . . ."

"Nay," said Emelius somberly. "Charon waits for all. Better to live well than to live long. I had not seen her since I was a child . . ." He sighed. "Every light has its shadow."

"And it's an ill wind—" began Charles eagerly.

Miss Price turned sharply. "What can you mean, Charles?"

"Nothing," said Charles. He looked a little shamefaced and stooped to pick up a stone.

"He's thinking of the house," said Carey. "Couldn't we go and see it?"

"Well, really, Carey—" began Miss Price. She seemed a little shocked.

"I mean, as we're so near? What's the good of going home? We'd only sit and mope. It might cheer him up," she added quickly. "I mean, it's his house now . . ."

"Would it yet be there?" asked Emelius.

Miss Price looked thoughtful. "I don't see why it shouldn't be." She turned to Emelius. "Do you know the way?"

Yes, he knew the way all right—none better— by Tinker's Lane. But this they found had become a cart track and disappeared into a farm. TRESPASSERS WILL BE PROSECUTED, said a notice on the gate, and a large black dog rushed out to bark at them.

"No matter," Emelius told them. Suddenly taking the lead, he led them back to the road, and, skirting the farm buildings, he took them through fields and spinneys to the base of the hill beyond. Miss Price became a little fussed and disheveled— she was not at her best climbing through hedges.

"Are you sure there isn't a bull?" she would ask, perched precariously on the upper rungs of a five-barred gate.

At last, they found the track again—a faint depression in the turfy grass. No more hedges; the hill swelled steeply above them. There were chalk and harebells and an occasional clump of beech trees. They followed the curve of the hill until at last the view widened beneath them and a sweet breeze stole their breath. Carey found a fossil; Miss Price mislaid a glove.

While they were searching, Emelius went ahead; turning a sudden corner, he seemed to disappear. When at last they came upon him, he was standing in a hollow, knee-deep in brambles. Among the brambles, there were stones and rubble. It might well have been the ruin of a house, Carey thought—looking about her—awash with elder bushes and trailing honeysuckle. Tears of disappointment came to her eyes. "Was it really here?" she asked, hoping he might be mistaken.

"Indeed, yes," Emelius assured her. He seemed elated rather than depressed—as though this was proof of his having skipped the centuries. He took Miss Price's hand and helped her down—quite excited he had become, almost boyish—and left her marooned on a piece of coping while gingerly he jumped from stone to stone, showing the general layout of the rooms. "Here was the parlor, here the dairy. This," he explained as he jumped down into a long hollow, "was the sunken garden where my aunt grew sweet herbs." He kicked the sandy rubble from some flat stones. "And here the cellar steps." He showed them where the apple orchard had been and the barn. "It was a comely, neat house," he repeated proudly. "And none to inherit it save I."

When they reached the main road, a strange incident occurred. Emelius disappeared. One moment he was walking just behind them, and the next he was nowhere to be seen. Miss Price stopped Dr. Lamond in his old Ford and asked him if he had seen, along the road, a young man of Emelius's description.

"Yes," said the doctor. "As I turned the corner, he was close behind you; then he made a dart for that field."

They found Emelius behind the hedge, white and shaking. It was the car that had unnerved him. His panic, in the face of such a monster, had left no place for courtesy. It was some time before Miss Price could calm him. When the mail van passed them later, Emelius stood his ground, but the sweat broke on his brow, and he quivered like a horse about to shy. He did not speak again until they reached home.

6

Magic in Moderation

Breaking Emelius into twentieth-century life was not easy, but Miss Price had great patience. He learned to clean his own shoes and to pass the bread and butter at tea. He became more modern in his speech, and once was heard to say okay. They had no sooner got him used to cars when he saw a jeep, and all their good work was undone. Airplanes he marveled at, but they did not come close enough to frighten him. But daily, as he learned more of the state of the world, modern inventions and the march of "progress," he clung closer to Miss Price as the one unassailable force in the midst of nightmarish havoc.

On warm evenings, after the children were in bed, he would be with Miss Price in the garden, stripping damsons with a rake (for bottling), and they would talk about magic. Carey could hear them through her window, their voices rising and falling in restrained but earnest argument as the damsons pattered into the basket and the sun sank low behind the trees. "I never scrape the scales from an adder," she once heard Miss Price say earnestly. "It takes force from any spell except those in which hemlock is combined with fennel. The only time I ever scrape the scales from an adder is in spells against Saint Vitus' dance; then, for some reason, it gives better results..." Sometimes, when Emelius had been speaking, Miss Price would exclaim rather scornfully, "Well, if you want to go back to the wax image and pin school—" and Carey always wondered what the wax image and pin school was, and why Emelius, having graduated, should want to go back there.

One evening Carey overheard a most curious conversation. It began by Miss Price saying brightly, "Have you ever tried intrasubstantiary locomotion?"

There was a mystified silence on the part of Emelius. Then he said, rather uncertainly, "No. At least, not often." (He had never confessed to Miss Price that, after a lifetime's study of magic, he had never yet got a spell to work.)

"It's awfully jolly," she went on. "I had a positive craze for it once." The damsons pattered gently into the basket, and Carey wondered if Emelius was as curious as she was.

Miss Price gave a little laugh. She sounded almost girlish. "Of course, as spells go, it's child's play. But sometimes the easiest things are the most effective, don't you think?"

Emelius cleared his throat. "I'm not sure that I haven't got it a little muddled in my mind," he ventured guardedly. "I may be confusing it with—"

Miss Price laughed quite gaily. "Oh, you couldn't confuse intrasubstantiary locomotion with anything else." She seemed amused.

"No," admitted Emelius. "No. I suppose you couldn't."

"Unless," said Miss Price, suddenly thoughtful, leaning forward on the rake and gazing earnestly into the middle distance, "you mean—"

"Yes," put in Emelius hastily, "that's what I do mean."

"What?" asked Miss Price wonderingly.

"That's what I was confusing it with."

"With what?"

"With—" Emelius hesitated. "With what you were going to say."

"But intrasubstantiary locomotion is *quite* different." Miss Price sounded surprised and rather puzzled.

"Oh, yes," admitted Emelius hastily, "it's completely different, but all the same—"

"You see, intrasubstantiary locomotion is making a pair of shoes walk without any feet in them."

"Ah, yes," agreed Emelius with relief. "*Shoes.* That's it."

"Or a suit of clothes get up and sit down."

"Yes," said Emelius, but he sounded a little less sure of himself.

"Of course," went on Miss Price enthusiastically, "the very best results are got from washing on a line." She laughed delightedly. "It's amazing what you can do with washing on a line."

"Astounding," agreed Emelius. He gave a nervous little laugh.

"Except sheets," Miss Price pointed out.

"Oh, sheets are no good."

"It has to be wearing apparel. Something you can make look as if a person was inside it."

"Naturally," said Emelius rather coldly.

At first Miss Price, anxious not to have him on her hands for too long, had taken great trouble to explain the circumstances that governed the length of Emelius's visit, but, latterly, as he began to settle down and find happiness in the discovery of friends, she, too, seemed sad at the thought of his departure. And contented as he was, he himself was a little worried about the Fire of London and what might have happened to his rooms in Cripplegate, and, also, he felt in duty bound (having read of his aunt's death in the churchyard) to attend to the business of inheriting her estate. "I can always come back and visit you," he would explain, "if you could come and fetch me."

But Miss Price didn't approve of this idea. "One thing or another," she would say, "not this dashing about between centuries. A settled life is good for everyone. I think the wise thing to do would be to give up your London establishment and settle down in your aunt's house at Pepperinge Eye. And we could walk up there sometimes, and it would be nice to think of your living there. You would not seem so far away."

Emelius thought this over. "It's a good piece of land," he said at last, but he spoke rather sadly.

Carey, who was present, said warmly, as if to comfort him, "We'd go there often. We'd sit on the stones in the parlor, near where the fireplace was, and we'd feel awfully near you—"

Emelius looked at her. "I'd like you to see the house," he said. "As it is in my day."

Carey turned to Miss Price.

"Couldn't we go just once?" she asked.

Miss Price tightened her lips. "It's always 'just once,' Carey. You've had your 'just once,' and we've still to take Mr. Jones back."

"If we promise not to stay a minute, just a second, when we take him back, couldn't we just go once and see him at his aunt's house?"

Emelius glanced at Miss Price's face, then sadly down at the lawn.

"It isn't," said Miss Price uncomfortably, "that I wouldn't be happy to go and see Mr. Jones, especially in that dear little house, but—"

"But what?" asked Carey.

"I'm responsible for you children. There seems to be no way of knowing what may happen on these outings—"

"Well," said Carey reasonably, "it's hardly much of an outing—just to go and visit Mr. Jones—in his quiet little house at Pepperinge Eye—not two miles away."

"I know, Carey," Miss Price pointed out. "But what about that quiet day we planned on the beach?"

"Well, after all, that was a cannibal island. This is quite different. Mr. Jones's aunt's dear little house. At Pepperinge Eye—"

"If you came just once," said Emelius. "Say, a week after I left, just to see it all. Then after that you could just come in spirit—"

"In spirit?" said Miss Price dubiously.

"I mean just take a walk up to where the house was and we'll think of each other," said Emelius.

Miss Price sat silent. They could not read her expression. At last she said, rather surprisingly, "I don't like flying in the face of nature—"

"Well," Carey pointed out, "isn't the broomstick—?"

"No," said Miss Price, "that's different, that's accepted—witches have always flown on broomsticks." She paused. "No, I don't quite know how to put it, and I don't really like to mention it, but there's no getting away from the fact that, as far as we're concerned, Mr. Jones is long since dead and buried."

Emelius stared glumly at the grass between his feet. He could not deny it.

"I don't hold it against him," went on Miss Price. "We must all come to it sooner or later, but it doesn't seem wise or natural to foster these attachments with one who is no more."

They sat silent; then, after a bit, Emelius sighed. "There is no record of my death in the churchyard," he pointed out.

Miss Price pursed up her lips. "That proves nothing. We did not look in the annex behind the yew hedge."

"Don't let's," said Carey suddenly.

7

A Change of Mind

But Miss Price stuck to the original plan. When Emelius's clothes arrived from the cleaners, they took him back. They dropped him in Goat Alley at night and did not stay a minute. Miss Price never liked long, drawn-out good-byes, and in her efforts to spare everybody's feelings she was almost too businesslike. She would not "step upstairs" to try his cherry cordial. She bundled the children back onto the bed with almost indecent haste, and left Emelius standing, somber and dark-robed, in the moonlit street. Embarrassed she seemed, and worried by the whole business, and she was sharp with the children when they got home, and next day flung herself into bottling as though she tried to drown the memory of that sad white face deep in sliced apricot and squashed tomato pulp. She did not join the children on their expeditions, and the bed-knob had been hidden away.

The happy atmosphere of the little house seemed to have dispersed, and the children wandered into the fields and sat on gates, talking and kicking their heels. They chewed long stalks of grass and quarreled idly, while the end of the holidays loomed in sight and lowered over them.

No one even mentioned Emelius until one day at tea when Miss Price, quite suddenly, brought the subject up herself.

"I wonder," she said, gazing pensively at the brown teapot, "if we should have taken Mr. Jones right home."

The atmosphere at once became electric. Carey laid down her teaspoon. All three pairs of eyes were fixed on Miss Price's face.

"But we did," said Charles after a moment.

"I mean," went on Miss Price, "leaving him in the street like that. It was rather rude."

"Yes," said Carey. "His house might have been damaged in the fire, or anything. He might have had nowhere to sleep that night."

Miss Price looked worried. "It was just that we agreed—didn't we?—not to stay."

"Yes," said Carey. "You remember we asked you whether if we promised not to stay a minute, a second, when we took him back, you would let us go later and visit him properly."

"I didn't promise anything," replied Miss Price hastily. She poured herself out another cup of tea. As she stirred it, she said uncertainly, "But I think he's all right, don't you? He could always go down to Pepperinge Eye."

"Yes," said Carey, "I'm sure he'd manage."

"And yet," went on Miss Price, "in some ways Mr. Jones is rather helpless. That fire, you know, they say there were riots afterward." Miss Price, without noticing what she was doing, put another spoonful of sugar in her tea.

"If one could write to him . . ." she suggested.

"Yes," said Carey, "but we can't."

Charles cleared his throat. "Would you like Paul and me just to run down and take a look at him?"

Carey opened her mouth. "Without me?" she said indignantly.

"No, no," put in Miss Price. "It wouldn't be fair to leave Carey. Perhaps—" She hesitated. "Perhaps we ought *all* to go."

The children were silent. They dared not urge her. Carey crossed her thumbs and stared fixedly at the tablecloth.

"We could just go to his lodgings and peep in at the window. Just to see if he's all right, don't you know. We wouldn't disturb him. I think," said Miss Price, "it would be *kind*."

The children did not speak.

"Once we knew he was all right," went on Miss Price, "we could come back and settle down happily to our lives."

"Yes," said Carey guardedly.

"Don't you think?" asked Miss Price.

"Oh, yes," said Charles.

"Although this is a flying visit," said Miss Price, "I think we should be prepared for any emergency." She took down her father's sword from its hook on the wall and tested the blade with her finger. Then she strapped the scabbard to the bed rail. Carey and Charles were folding blankets, and Paul was opening out the groundsheet. It was nine o'clock in the morning, and they were all gathered together in Miss Price's bedroom to prepare for the journey.

"You see," went on Miss Price, "although I'm now convinced it is our duty to go, it is a great responsibility for me, now, at the end of the holidays. I don't feel justified in taking risks. I'm not sure that we shouldn't be disguised—"

"How do you mean?" asked Charles.

"We look so very twentieth century," said Miss Price. "And it will be daylight this time."

"I know!" exclaimed Carey. "Let's hire something from a costumer, like we did for the school play."

"No, no," said Miss Price. "I couldn't go in fancy dress. I shouldn't feel myself at all—but I have that black cloak, and you children would be all right in long dressing gowns, pinned up at the neck."

"Oh, Miss Price, that wouldn't look like *anything*. The costumer would have the exact dress. I have seven and sixpence."

"It would cost more than seven and sixpence," said Miss Price. "And we're only going to stay ten minutes. Dressing gowns are good enough. You are always apt to overdo things, Carey, and become fantastic. Now help me turn the mattress."

"I should think," said Carey, taking hold of the mattress, "we should look jolly fantastic walking about London in Charles II's reign wearing twentieth-century dressing gowns pinned up at the neck—"

"Now, Carey, that's enough. I have not the remotest intention of walking about London, and you're very lucky to be going at all."

8

So Near

Emelius opened his eyes. Then he closed them again. The light hurt them. "It is a dream," he told himself, "a nightmare, the worst I have ever had." He felt cold, but too bruised and tired to mind that he felt cold. He just lay there, on the stone floor, trying not to wake up. But, after a while, his eyes seemed to open of their own accord, and he saw the small, barred window and the gray sky beyond. He sat up suddenly, and then cried out with pain as the movement hurt him. He smelled the wetness of his clothes, and his hands slipped on the floor. Slowly he began to remember: yesterday, the horsepond; today, the stake. . . .

He had been betrayed. During the Fire of London men had lost their heads. A papist plot, they said, had caused it, and Frenchmen had thrown fireballs to burn the city. Somebody had spoken of Emelius, who lived so mysteriously in his dim lodging off Goat Alley, and king's men had searched his dwelling. There they found evidence of witchcraft and of sorcery, and when, on his return, he had walked up the dark stairway, two men had met him at the head and another, appearing from nowhere, cut off his retreat at the foot. He had been thrown into prison and tried, so angry were the people, almost immediately. When it was proved that he was no Frenchman, nor implicated in any "papist" plot, they accused him of having helped to cause the fire by magic. It was strange, they said, how he had left the city just before and returned when danger was over, and that his house, in the midst of such destruction, was barely touched.

Ah, the horsepond...that was terror! One little boy he remembered, a little boy with bare feet, who had run along beside him, ahead of the crowd, as they half dragged, half carried him toward the pond; a little brown-faced boy who shouted and jeered, showing his white teeth, and who stooped every few moments to pick a stone out of the dust. Emelius would try to duck, to shy away from that stone when it came singing through the air. He felt the little boy's laughing delighted face as part of the pain when the stone cut his cheek or glanced off his head.

And the tying of his hands and feet, the constable standing by, the clergyman's solemn face. And then the sickening plunge downward to the green water, the floating duckweed... a little parchment boat, half soaked, caught on a twig... and then the choking, greenish darkness... a noise in his ears like a scale played quickly on a violin. If he sank and died there in the water, it showed he was a human man and innocent of magic, but if he lived, that was a sign that he lived by supernatural powers, and they would burn him at the stake.

Then up he had come, choking, spluttering, coughing. The thick robe, tied at the ankles, had held the air. He saw the sunlight and heard the frightened quack of ducks. Then down, down again, into the water... the singing in his ears, the blackness; a blackness that thickened and spread, calming his fear, blotting out his thoughts.

And now it was morning. He had lain all night where they had thrown him on the cold floor. Cold... yes, he was cold, right through to the kernel of his heart, but he would not be cold for long; soon his wet clothes would steam; he would feel the hot steam rise upward past his face, and then his clothes would smolder; he would feel the heat of their smoldering against his skin, and their dry smoke in his nostrils—then, suddenly, the clothes would flare up into a running flame....

The stake... it was years since they had burned

anyone at the stake. Witches and sorcerers were hanged nowadays, not burned. It was barbarous, monstrous, to burn a man alive! But the people were obsessed today by fire, fire, fire....

"Oh," cried Emelius, putting his hands on his closed eyelids. "The stake...the stake...save me from the stake!"

He sat quiet, his face hidden in his hands, as though, if he were still enough, he might find that, after all, he had died there in the horsepond and it was all over. "Here I am," he thought bitterly, "condemned for witchcraft, and I never knew a spell that worked."

If it had been Miss Price—that would have been fairer; she was a witch, a real one, but no one would dare burn her. No one would pull Miss Price out of her tidy little house and drag her down the High Street to the village green. If she paid her taxes, observed the English Sunday, and worked for the Red Cross, no one bothered what she did with the rest of her time. She could create a black cat as big as an elephant, and no one would molest her as long as she kept it off other people's property and did not ill-treat it.

"Oh, Miss Price, if you knew—" groaned Emelius, his eyes hidden, "if you knew that I am to be burned at the stake!"

"I do know," said a voice. "They told me at your lodging."

Emelius slowly drew his fingers from his eyes. He stared round the cell. It was empty.

His fear, perhaps, was turning him crazy. The voice had seemed real, not very loud, and quite matter-of-fact. And then he saw her—a face at the window, and two hands with whitened knuckles grasping the bars. The face stared at him from under a black cowl, and, at first, he did not recognize the shadowed eye sockets and the lips compressed with effort, but then the long nose leaped, as it were, into his fear-dimmed vision, a pink-tipped banner of indignation and righteous wrath.

"Such a time getting here," she complained testily. "Asking, asking. And such rudeness."

Still Emelius did not speak. He was shivering as if, suddenly, he had come alive to the cold.

"Not a soul that seems to understand the king's English," went on the angry voice. She was panting slightly as if she held herself up by her own efforts. "I don't see how you've stood it. And the dirt, the untidiness, the smells ... but we won't go into that now—" She slipped out of sight with a sharp exclamation. Then, after a moment, she appeared again. "Lost my foothold," she explained. "I'm in a very awkward position. But you're locked in, and there's no room for the bed."

Emelius moistened his lips with his tongue. His eyes were fixed on the face at the window.

"They swam me in the horsepond," he moaned, as if he were talking to himself. "In the horse-pond—"

"Well, never mind," said Miss Price briskly. "Don't dwell on it!" She looked down, and Emelius heard her say indistinctly, "Well, move your finger, Carey. It's your own fault. I didn't mean to tread on it." There was a pause, then he heard Miss Price say, "Yes, he's all right. Very wet. But the cell's too small for the bed." She peered in at him. "Just a minute," she said, and disappeared.

He heard the gentle sound of voices. He lay back. Thankfulness crept up from his toes, up and up, until his heart swelled from it, and it forced tears from his eyes—hot painful tears that squeezed out from between his closed lids. Miss Price was here. She would save him. Miss Price never undertook a thing she did not finish, and Miss Price did everything so well.

After a while she appeared again. "Now," she said, "you must pull yourself together. We're not going to let you be burned, but we can't stay here.

It's broad daylight, and I'm standing on the bed rail—"

"Don't go!" begged Emelius.

"I must go, for the moment, and find a place for the bed. There's going to be a storm. And it was such nice weather when we left home."

"What shall I do?" gasped Emelius.

"There's nothing for you to do at the moment, and there are two men at the main door playing dice. You must keep calm and try not to fuss." She looked at him speculatively. "Tidy yourself up a bit and you'll feel better." Then, once more, she disappeared.

This time she did not come back, and, after a while, Emelius, because Miss Price had told him to, began picking long strands of green slime off his fur-trimmed robe. He found a water beetle up his sleeve, and his shoes were full of mud. Yes, she would save him, but how? It was not going to be easy. The barred window, sunk deep in the wall, was only a foot square, and the locked door was made of iron.

9

And Yet So Far

"She's an awful long time coming," said Carey.

The three children sat on the bed in a disused cow byre. The ground was trodden and dusty, and a pile of grayish hay rotted in the corner. Through the broken door they could see a bleak field below a dark and lowering sky. It was a dismal place but, as Miss Price had pointed out, a secluded one in which to hide the bed. She had gone off, wrapped in her black cloak, broomstick in one hand and sword in the other, to see what could be done for Emelius.

"She's been gone an hour, about," said Charles, walking to the door. The dark sky had a whitish streak in it, which shed an unreal, livid light on the trees and hedges. There was a sudden quivering brightness. Charles dodged back as a rumbling arch of thunder unrolled itself above the roof. "It startled me," he said.

"Do you think we ought to go and look for her?" asked Carey.

"What about the bed? Someone ought to stay and watch it."

"Nobody will come here," said Carey. "They're all gone to the burning. I think that we ought all to go or *all* to stay. Not split up."

Charles looked thoughtfully across the field toward the gate that led into the road. "Let's all go then," he said.

At the doorway Carey glanced back at the bed. It stood incongruously bright, with its legs sunk deep in dust and broken straw. "I wonder if we shall see it again," she thought to herself. "I wonder what we are letting ourselves in for."

As they walked along, in the gloomy light, between the uneven houses and their deserted gardens, they looked around them curiously. It was not very different from parts of England they knew. New houses squatted beside old ones. An inn sign creaked in a sudden gust of wind, but the inn was deserted. Everyone had gone to the burning.

"Smithfield," said Charles, "where the meat market is. It's really part of London, but it looks like country."

Horses and carts were tethered to posts. There were a great many half-starved cats about and rough-coated, mangy-looking dogs, which ran slyly down the alleyways, but there were no people. Old bones and rags and broken pan lids lay in the gutters, and there was a strong smell of tanning. As they walked, they began to hear the murmur of a crowd.

"Look!" said Carey in a low voice.

A richly dressed man was leading a horse out of a stable yard. He wore leather boots or leggings, which came up to his thighs, and a skirted coat. Lace fell over his wrists as far as his knucklebones, and a great dark wig moved heavily on his shoulders. As they came abreast of him, they smelled his perfume, a strange, rich, spicy smell, which mingled oddly with the stench of the tannery. Preparing to mount, he stared at them wonderingly. His pale face was full of disapproval. Carey nervously put up her hand to cover her safety pin, but he was not looking at their clothes. Something deeper seemed to worry him. "A poor wretch burned at the stake," he said as they passed close beside him, "a fine sight for children!"

Carey stared back at him with frightened eyes. She felt as you always feel when a complete stranger speaks to you angrily. As the clatter of his hooves died away behind them, the children walked in silence. They felt guilty, as if it were their fault that Emelius was to be burned alive.

Then suddenly the road opened into a square, or green, and they came upon the crowd. It was like a painting Carey had seen somewhere, or like a historical film, except it was more colorful than a painting and dirtier than a historical film. Boys had climbed trees and railings; every window was full of people. Above the babble of talk certain voices were heard calling some indistinct, monotonous phrase. Carey jumped when just behind her a woman yodeled:

"Fair lemons and oranges.
Oranges and citrons."

They could get in no closer. They were jammed close beside a fat woman with three children and what seemed to be the railings of a cattle pen. The fat woman, who wore a white cap round her red face, with a hat on top of it, was breaking a cake for her children. It smelled of cinnamon and made Carey feel hungry.

Carey put her foot on the bottom rail of the cattle pen and pushed herself up between the knees of the boys who sat on top of it. Ah, now she could see the stake! It was raised only a little above the crowd. Two men with muskets slung on their backs were busy with ropes. When they moved aside, she saw Emelius, a limp, sagged figure. He was tied round

205

the chest. She could not see any lower than his knees. She could not see the fagots. There was no sign of Miss Price.

Charles climbed up beside her. She heard him exclaim when he saw Emelius, and then Paul was pulling at the skirt of her dressing gown.

"Could I have a toffee apple?" he said.

Carey stepped down. Paul was too young to see Emelius burn, or even be told about it. "We haven't any money, Paul," Carey explained kindly, "to buy toffee apples," but she looked round and there indeed was a woman with a tray slung round her neck selling toffee apples right and left—toffee apples and lollipops on sticks. The woman with the three children gave Paul a piece of cinnamon cake. She stared at them curiously. "She notices our clothes," thought Carey.

Then a hush fell on the crowd. Someone up near the stake was speaking, but they could not see him, nor hear what he said. "They're going to start soon," announced Charles from his perch on the railing. Carey saw a thin trail of smoke. She climbed up beside Charles again to see, but it was only a man with a spluttering torch, which he held aloft as if waiting for an order. Someone else was speaking now. Carey glimpsed a long form in black, a lawyer, perhaps, or a clergyman.

The figure at the stake still sagged, the head hanging forward on the chest. "Miss Price ... Miss Price ..." breathed Carey, clinging to the rail. "Save him. Oh please, save poor Emelius."

The voice finished speaking. The crowd became terribly silent. Other people tried to climb on the railing. All eyes were turned toward the stake. Suddenly there was a roll of drums. The man with the torch circled it about his head and flung it downward, in amongst the fagots.

Carey shrieked and jumped down off the railing, hiding her eyes. The roll of drums went on, swelling in intensity. Clouds of smoke rose up against the dark and threatening sky. A quivering flash and, for one livid second, the whole scene stood etched in lightning—lightning that played in forks across the gloomy sky—then the sound of drums was drowned in a crashing, earsplitting roll of thunder, roaring and trembling across the heavens until it seemed to shake the very earth on which they stood.

Then Carey heard shrieks and cries. She clambered, pushing for a foothold, upon the railing to see what had happened. Something seemed to be bending the crowd like a field of corn in wind, something of which they seemed afraid. The shrieks of the women shrilled and multiplied. There was a movement of pushing, of fighting, of panic. Carey pulled

Paul beside her close against the railing. Paul began to cry.

"Charles," cried Carey, her voice breaking with excitement. "Look! Look!"

Something was skimming low over the crowd, a great black bird it seemed, which flew in narrowing circles and whose passage seemed to cut a swath in the frightened mob as it passed, as hair falls aside from the comb.

"It's she! It's Miss Price!" cried Carey. "Paul, it's Miss Price! Charles . . ."

People were pushing, screaming, rushing to get out of reach. Now, it was coming toward their corner, swooping low and steady on its curving flight. The fat woman shrieked and ran, dragging her children after her. The boys jumped down off the railing. "A witch, a witch!" they screamed hoarsely. "A witch on a broomstick!"

But Carey and Charles, holding Paul tight against them, kept their places. They gazed upward with anxious eyes at the black and fluttering figure that came toward them in the gloom. Shrouded and unrecognizable, it swept past, and an eerie wail, thin and terrifying, trailed behind it on the wind.

People had run away, down the side streets, down the alleys. There were spaces of empty trodden grass and littered dusty ground. A basket seller was collecting his stock, which rolled around in every direction, but he dropped it all again as the dark figure flew near him and ran "hell for leather" for the entrance of a tavern.

Now the children could see the stake quite clearly. The smoke had cleared, and red tongues of flame, licking their way upward through the fagots, shone weirdly in the leaden gloom. Emelius, bound round the chest and ankles, hung forward on his ropes.

"He's catching fire!" shrieked Carey. "Oh, Miss Price, hurry, hurry!"

Soldiers, who had acted as a cordon against the crowd, formed a group, training their muskets on the broomstick's flight. Only one remained beside the stake, and he seemed to be charging his gun, looking up fearfully from time to time as if he feared the dark swooping figure might come upon him from behind.

"Perhaps she's forgotten," Charles reminded Carey fearfully. "She burned the books."

There was a report, which echoed back against the houses. One of the soldiers had fired. Once more the lightning flashed, and thunder pealed across the angry sky. The square was empty now, save for the soldiers and the huddled group of children beside the cattle pen. The ground was scattered with litter. Benches, chairs, and stools—things that people had brought to stand on—lay overturned and broken.

As the flying figure approached the stake, the remaining soldier fled to join the others, clutching his musket. The broomstick and the sweeping black cloak seemed almost to touch the burning fagots when the children saw a sword flash.

"It's her father's sword," exclaimed Charles excitedly. "She's going to cut him free."

Carey was reminded, watching the awkward efforts to bring the broomstick within striking distance yet not too close, of a left-handed golfer trying to play polo.

"Oh, dear," she cried in an agony of fear. "She'll cut his head off."

Emelius, aware at last, twisted and leaned and strained at his cords in terrified efforts to escape the deadly thrusts. A gust of spark-filled smoke blew against his face, and the children saw him coughing. Still the attack continued.

"Careful," she shouted. "Please, oh please, Miss Price!"

Again there was a report, followed immediately by two others. The soldiers were firing. Carey, glancing fearfully at the bell-mouthed weapons, wondered how such guns could miss.

"They've got her," said Charles then, in his most reserved voice.

"No," cried Carey wildly, "no, they can't have!"

Her eyes flew back to the stake, and she covered her mouth quickly to hold back a scream.

The broomstick was poised, motionless, shuddering, above the crackling wood. The sword dropped and stuck upright, quivering among the fagots. The broomstick wavered and sank downward toward the smoke and flame. Then, as they watched, painfully it seemed to pull itself free. It rose a little and made a limping, hesitating flight toward the head of a road leading out of the square. The soldiers turned slowly, keeping the fluttering object covered with their guns. Figures appeared in doorways. Several men, braver than the others, ventured into the street. All eyes were fixed on the black and tattered object that rose a little and then sank once more toward the ground, in painful hopping flight.

The children no longer watched the stake, where each second for Emelius became uncomfortably warmer; their eyes were fixed on the broomstick. They gripped each other in an agony of fear. Nothing seemed to matter in the world except Miss Price and her safety. As they watched, the broomstick rose a little. Jerkily swaying, rather drunkenly, as if it had lost its sense of direction, it made off down the street, at about the level of the first-floor windows.

Then a man threw a brick, and the soldiers fired again. The broomstick stopped in midair.

For about the twentieth part of a second the children saw the folds of the black cloak hang limp, before the whole equipage dropped like a stone. Then they could see it no more. People ran out of doorways, out of yards, out of alleys. Some were armed with staves, some with clubs; they saw one man, a butcher he must have been, with a large and shining chopper. All these people made for the spot where the broomstick had fallen. The narrow mouth of the street was choked with an ever-increasing crowd, composed mostly of boys and men. No one glanced at the stake or felt the sudden onslaught of the rain. It poured down suddenly, a slanting rushing sheet of water, mingling with the tears on Carey's face and turning the churned dust into mud.

"Miss Price . . . Miss Price . . ." sobbed Carey, while the rain ran down her hair into the neck of her dressing gown. She hardly noticed Charles had left her side. She did not know how he had got there when she saw him clamber on the steaming fagots, which hissed and blackened under the downpour. She watched Charles seize the sword and chop at the ropes that bound Emelius. She saw Emelius fall forward on the piled wood, and the wood roll from under him. She saw Emelius hit the ground, and Charles climbing down from the stake, sword in hand. She saw Emelius picking himself up from the ground in a dazed way, his charred robe hanging in strips about his yellow-stockinged legs. She saw Charles urging him, talking to him, pulling him by the arm. Then Charles and Emelius were there beside her where she leaned with Paul against the cattle pen. Charles was pulling off Emelius's coat, so that he stood in shirt and breeches and wrinkled yellow stockings. . . .

"Miss Price, Miss Price . . ." Carey went on sobbing.

"They won't recognize you so easily like that," Charles was explaining to Emelius. "You're not a bit burnt. Lucky your clothes were so wet. Come, Carey," he went on, looking white but determined. "Do shut up, we've got to get back to the bed."

"But Miss Price—" cried Carey wildly. "We can't leave Miss Price."

"We must," said Charles. "There's nothing we can do now. She would want us to be sensible."

Paul began to bellow loudly. He had no inhibitions. If Miss Price was dead, he was not going to be brave. Paul's noise had a steadying effect on Carey; she took his hand. "Quiet, Paul," she said, sniffing. "We can cry when we get home."

They could not walk quickly because Charles had burned his feet. Perhaps it was just as well; running might have aroused suspicion. Emelius seemed in a dream. He did not speak and gazed before him as if he still saw a black figure fluttering wildly on a broomstick. As they neared the gate leading into the field, the same fear descended on all of them. Suppose the bed had gone. . . .

Carey and Paul had dropped a little behind, and it was Charles who entered the cowshed first. When Carey heard him exclaim, she deliberately stood still—waiting there in the squishy grass while the rain poured down. She felt she couldn't bear much more.

"Carey!" Charles was shouting. "Carey! Come and see!"

Carey dragged herself to the door of the cowshed. At first, in the gloom, she could see nothing. Then she distinguished the outline of the bed. A figure was lying on it—a figure propped up on one elbow—and a pair of angry eyes met her own in a stare of baleful accusation.

"Oh, Miss Price!" cried Carey. She clutched at the doorpost, as if she might have fallen.

"You may well look guilty," scolded Miss Price. Even in that light the tip of her nose was an angry pink. "You are the most thoughtless and untrustworthy children. I distinctly told you to stay by the bed. I've been frightened out of my wits about you. Out of my wits. I come back here, worn-out with

witchcraft, longing to put my feet up for five minutes—and what do I find?"

"Oh!" cried Carey. She rushed across the cowshed. She flung herself upon the bed. She sobbed
down Miss Price's neck as if her heart would break.

"There!" said Miss Price uncomfortably, patting
Carey's shoulder blades. "There! No need to get
emotional. We've all been a little upset, that's what
it is."

"You're safe," gasped Carey. "Darling Miss
Price. They didn't kill you."

Miss Price drew her head away as if she were
surprised. "Kill me?" she exclaimed, with something like horror. She stared at them unbelievingly.
"Gracious goodness alive, you didn't imagine that
was me on the broomstick?"

"Then what was it, Miss Price?" asked poor
Carey, wiping her eyes. "Whatever was it?"

Miss Price stared at her a moment longer, then
she gave a little triumphant glance in the direction
of Emelius. "That," she said, blushing slightly, "was
just a particularly apposite use of intrasubstantiary
locomotion."

But Emelius, stretched out wearily on the hay in
the corner, did not even look up.

10

And Farther Still

Emelius was put to bed in Charles's room and remained there several days. He was suffering, Miss Price said, from "shock." Charles's feet were more scorched than burnt, and some yellow ointment spread on gauze soon healed them. In a week's time the vacation would be over, and Miss Price was gentler, kinder to them than they had ever known her. She spent her time between packing for the children and arranging trays for Emelius. She was so kind, so unusually long-suffering, that the children were a little afraid. They thought Emelius must be worse than Miss Price had at first supposed. Several times Carey saw a strange man in the house, and it was not always the same one. Once Miss Price came downstairs with two of them at her heels. All three went into the dining room and closed the door, and, for over an hour, the house felt tense with mystery. She seemed, too, to be writing a lot of letters and running off down to the village to telephone. But instead of getting fussed, she became kinder and kinder. They didn't like it at all and were filled with dread when, on the last day of the holidays, she summoned them rather solemnly into the sitting room, where, since Emelius came, Charles had been sleeping.

The three children sat on Charles's bed, and Miss Price, facing them, took a little upright chair. There was a feeling of great tenseness in the air.

Miss Price cleared her throat and clasped her hands together in her lap.

"Children," she said, "what I am going to tell you will not come altogether as a surprise. You have noticed a good deal of coming and going in the house during this past week and must have gathered something was afoot."

Miss Price moistened her lips with her tongue and clasped her hands a little tighter together. The children's eyes watched every movement, seeking some hint of what was going to come.

"I do not possess anything of great value," went on Miss Price, "but my belongings, such as they are, are in excellent repair. The kitchen sink, put in only last year, cost me, with the labor, nearly fifty pounds, but I shall not leave the bathroom fittings. It was a help to me, in making my decision, to remember that I could take these with me. If I have a weakness, and we all have many, it is a weakness for modern plumbing. I've nothing against the Simple Life, assuming that there is such a thing, but bathing in a washtub is so unnecessarily complicated." Miss Price paused.

"The proceeds will go to the Red Cross," she added.

Carey leaned forward. She seemed to hesitate a moment, and then she said, "What proceeds, Miss Price?"

"I keep telling you, Carey. The proceeds from the sale of the house."

"You're going to sell the house!"

"Carey, try to pay more attention when people are speaking to you. I'm selling the house and the furniture, except, as I say, the bathroom fittings."

"And you're giving the money to the Red Cross?"

"Every penny."

"Why?" asked Charles.

"To compensate this century for the loss of an able-bodied woman."

Carey began to smile. She half stood up and then sat down again. "I see," she said slowly. "Oh, Miss Price—"

"I don't see," complained Charles.

"Charles," said Carey, turning to him eagerly.

"It's sort of good and bad news. Miss Price means—"
She looked at Miss Price uncertainly. "I think Miss
Price means—"

Miss Price made her face quite expressionless.
She cleared her throat. "Perhaps I didn't make it
quite clear, Charles," she conceded, "that Mr. Jones
has asked me to share his life." She allowed Charles
a small and dignified smile. "And I have accepted."

Charles stared. He looked completely bewildered. "You're going to live in the seventeenth
century?"

"Of necessity," said Miss Price. "Mr. Jones can't
stay here, and, there, we have a house and livestock,
an orchard—and Mr. Jones has a little something
laid by."

"But how will you go?" asked Charles. "Unless
Paul comes too?"

"It's all arranged. Mr. Bisselthwaite will call for
you tomorrow morning and will put you on the train.
And this evening, after supper, Paul will stand on
the floor near the head of the bed and twist the
knob."

"You're going tonight?" exclaimed Charles.

"Unfortunately we must. I dislike doing things
in a hurry, but, without Paul, we have no means of
conveyance."

Carey turned sideways, so that she lay on one

elbow. She picked some fluff off the blanket, staring closely at her hand.

"Miss Price—" she said.

"Well?"

"Will you—" Carey stared hard at the blanket. "Will you like it?"

Miss Price lifted her hands and let them fall on the arms of the chair. Strangely enough she did not, as Carey expected, have an answer ready.

"Mr. Jones and I," said Miss Price slowly, gazing at the wall as if she could see through it, "are two lonely people. We shall be better together."

"The bed can never come back," said Charles.

Miss Price, gazing at the wall, did not reply.

Once again there was a faint film of dust (and two feathers) where the bed had stood. But this time the room looked barer still, with the rugs rolled up and the dressing-table drawers left slightly open. A crumpled piece of tissue flew lightly across the room and caught itself against the leg of the washstand.

She had gone. Where a minute before there had been bustle and flurry, tyings-up and tuckings-in, hurried good-byes and last-minute hugs, there was silence and emptiness.

The bed had been dangerously overloaded. The

bathroom plumbing, dissected amateurishly by Charles and Emelius, and wrapped in ironing blankets and dust sheets, took up so much room to start with. And then, besides the clothes basket and two suitcases there were the last-minute things that Miss Price could not bear to leave behind. The silver cream jug, her extra hot-water bottle, an egg-beater, a cake tin tied with string in which she had put her store of tea, some biscuits, a packet of Ryvita, and six tins of sardines. There were her apostle spoons and the best tea cloth, her father's sword, her photographs, a bottle of lavender water. . . . They had tied and retied it all with the clothesline, but, all the same, it looked terribly perilous with Miss Price and Emelius perched on top. In spite of everything, Carey pointed out, Miss Price would wear her best straw hat, which had been "done over" by a woman in the village. "Better to wear it than pack it," she had insisted, as if there had been no other alternative. She had cried a little when she said goodbye to the children and reminded them that Mrs. Kithatten down the road was coming in to cook their breakfast; and that their tickets were on the mantelpiece in the dining room; and that Mr. Bisselthwaite would be there by nine-thirty; and to remind Mrs. Kithatten that the men would be along any time after one to check on the inventory; and that they were to boil up the rest of the milk in case it turned before morning.

And then Paul had wished, standing there beside the bedstead, and, suddenly, the room was empty, except for the rustling tissue paper and the curtains falling softly back in place as if there had been a wind.

They felt terribly alone. They went downstairs, and the emptiness of the house seemed to follow them. They walked through the kitchen into the scullery. The drainboard was still damp from the washing up of the supper things, a washing up Miss Price had shared. The door of the garden stood open, and they wandered out. There, by the garbage can, stood a pile of Miss Price's old shoes. One pair, very stiff and mud-caked, were the ones she kept for gardening in wet weather.

The sun was sinking behind the wood, but the hillside was bathed in golden light.

"They'll be there by now," Charles said at last, breaking the dreary silence.

Carey looked across the shadowed wood to the familiar, friendly slope of Tinker's Hill.

"I know what," she exclaimed suddenly. "Let's run up there! We'll be back before dark."

"Well, we wouldn't see them or anything," objected Charles.

"It doesn't matter. Miss Price might sort of know."

It was good to run and climb, panting, up the sandy paths, through the bracken, onto the turf. It was good to reach the wind and feel the sunshine as, rich and warm, it fell on their shoulders and sent long shadows bobbing on ahead across the grass.

When they reached the ruined house, Carey climbed alone to the highest spot on the wall. She sat with her chin in her hands, as if in a trance, while the wind blew the wisps of hair on her forehead and her motionless shadow stretched out across the blackberry bushes and up the sun-drenched hill. Charles and Paul just messed about among the stones, uneasily picking an occasional blackberry and watching Carey.

After a while Carey climbed down. She did not speak. She walked slowly past the boys. There was a faraway expression on her face, and her eyes were dreamy.

"I can see them," she said in a chanting kind of voice. She stood quite still, among the brambles of the "apple orchard."

"Oh, come on, Carey," said Charles. He knew she was acting, but all the same he did not like it.

"I can see them quite plainly," went on Carey, as if she had not heard. She stretched out her hands in a hushing gesture and raised her face a little, like a picture they had at home called "The Prophetess." "They are walking slowly down the path, hand in hand." She paused. "Now, they have stopped under the apple tree. Miss Price has no hat on. Now they have turned and are looking back at the house—"

"Oh, Carey, come on," said Charles uncomfortably. "It's getting dark."

"Now," Carey dropped her voice respectfully, "Mr. Jones has kissed Miss Price on the cheek. He's saying—" Carey paused, as if thinking up the words. "He is saying," she went on triumphantly, " 'My own true love . . .' "

Then suddenly Charles and Paul saw Carey's expression change. Her eyes widened and her mouth dropped open. She looked round hurriedly, then she ran, almost leaped out of the brambles, and clambered awkwardly upon the wall. She stared downward at the spot where she had stood.

"What's the matter, Carey? What happened?" cried Charles.

Carey's face was pale. She looked unnerved, but somewhere about her mouth was the shadow of a smile.

"Didn't you hear?" she asked.

"No," said Charles, "I didn't hear anything."

"Didn't you hear Miss Price?"

"*Really* Miss Price!"

"Yes. It was her voice. Quite loud and distinct."

Charles and Paul looked grave.

"What—what did she say?" stammered Charles.

"She said, 'Carey, come at once out of those lettuces.' "

Mary Norton (1903–1992) lived in England, where she was an actress, playwright, and award-winning author. As a child she created a make-believe world in which tiny people inhabited the hedgerows, living their lives out of the sight of humans. It is from this private fantasy that her most well-known books, those about the Borrowers, came about. But before she wrote *The Borrowers,* she wrote two enormously popular books, *The Magic Bed-Knob* and *Bonfires and Broomsticks,* which were later combined into the present volume.